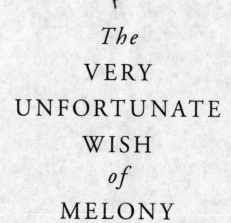

The
VERY
UNFORTUNATE
WISH
of
MELONY
YOSHIMURA

Also by
WAKA T. BROWN

While I Was Away
Dream, Annie, Dream

WAKA T. BROWN

the
VERY
UNFORTUNATE
WISH of
MELONY
YOSHIMURA

Quill Tree Books
An Imprint of HarperCollins Publishers

For my children,
who have endured
so much these
past few years.

I love you
to the moon and
back . . . to infinity
times infinity. . . .

But this doesn't mean
you can skip
your morning chores.

Chapter ONE

Once upon a time
In a small Japanese village
(Oh no . . .)
There was an old man and woman
Who wanted a child more than anything else in the world.
(Here we go again.)
They prayed and wished and prayed some more
Until one day, a melon came bobbing and floating down the
river.
(I've heard this so many times. They know I've heard this
before.)
The old woman brought it home.
(Why are they torturing me like this?)
When she cut it open,
There was a baby inside.
(Please don't say it. PLEASE.)

And they named her Melony!
(Of course they said it. They always do.
Why did I think this time would be any different?
Don't roll your eyes. DON'T roll
them. . . .)

very. Single. Time.

For as long as I could remember, on every momentous occasion, my parents busted out this ridiculous story about how I was born from a melon.

I'd always been able to control my reactions before—I'm not sure why today was different. But my parents acted like they didn't see the eye roll so massive that it almost pulled me off my chair. They pretended not to hear my sigh so huge it could have blown out all the candles on my birthday cake.

To be fair, it wasn't just because of my parents and their silly story.

It also was because I had checked the mailbox *and* my email a total of three times each so far, and there wasn't anything from my best friend, Louisa Lyons. Nothing from Sophia or Olivia either. No big surprise there, but Louisa . . . we'd been friends since kindergarten. It had already been a month since she and her family had left for their grand, year-long RV adventure across the US that would eventually end at their new home in sunny Arizona. She didn't send a card—not a message, not even a "HBD" text. But maybe there would have been if I had a real phone. Which I don't. Not yet, anyway.

"I can't believe you're twelve already," my mom sighed along after me. "Not a little girl anymore."

"Sure she is!" My dad interrupted my mom's musings. "Still shorter than me. But anyway, she used to be such a handful. She's much better now, sou darou?"

My mom brightened at the memories. "Sou ne! Little Uriko was like a storm."

"Like hail in summer!" my dad laughed.

"Remember when she used to run around and climb trees and chase bees suppadaka—what's that in English?" my mom asked.

"Stark naked!" Dad responded.

Okay, this is really getting out of hand. Not only did my mom call me by the Japanese name I discarded when I was five, but now she's learned the phrase "stark naked" and will likely use it any chance she gets.

But I guess she doesn't go out all that much, so I probably didn't need to worry.

"I should blow the candles out before they melt." I directed their focus back to the beautiful cake in front of us. We didn't have dessert very often, and cake even less, so it was easy getting my parents to stop talking about what a wild kid I used to be and turn their attention back to our celebration.

"That's right!" My parents gently pushed the cake closer to me and wished me happy birthday in Japanese. "Otanjoubi omedetou!"

I took a deep breath and held it for a moment as I thought about what to wish for. And then let all the air out in a *whoosh*. The flames flickered and danced, but in the end they were no match for me. Thin wisps of smoke floated up toward our dark-wooden-beamed ceiling.

My mom immediately plucked the candles from the cake and dropped them in a glass of water. Then she carefully fished them out and dried them on a napkin so we could use them for my birthday next year. "So, what did you wish for?"

"She can't tell you that!" my dad answered for me.

"Why not?"

"Because then it won't come true."

"Hmmm . . . is that what Americans believe?"

This skepticism from a woman who still insists I was born from a melon.

My parents didn't celebrate birthdays with cake when they were little kids in Japan, so my mom improvised. Every year it was the same type of cake for my birthday. Golden sponge cake from the store that she layered with defrosted frozen strawberries because it was impossible to find fresh ones in the fall. She made a syrup from them, too, by mashing up the berries and blending with a little honey. After that, she covered it all in lightly sweetened, vanilla-scented whipped cream and decorated with more fruit on top—usually sliced kiwis and mandarin orange segments, mangoes if there were any ripe ones.

"Are your friends' cakes like this?" she asked the first time she made it.

I didn't have much of a filter when I was little, but even then I knew not to say, "Nah, Louisa's mom and dad get a big cake from Costco, and the person behind the counter writes 'Happy Birthday!' in dark blue frosting from a tube."

Besides, my mom's improvised cake was pretty tasty, too, with its strawberries that soaked into the tender sponge and the tartness of the fruit mixed with the creamy topping. Even though I knew she added the fruit to make it healthy, I devoured it in no seconds flat.

Because the sooner I was finished, the sooner I could open my presents.

It didn't matter, though, because my parents chose to "savor" the cake instead. Mom made sure to give me a slice that was twice as large as theirs, but they still took three times as long to finish.

"It's like eating a cloud mixed with sunshine," my dad complimented my mom.

"Pssh," Mom responded. She isn't comfortable with compliments. That's probably why she doesn't give out many herself.

When they finally finished and my dad had cleared the table (usually my chore, but not on my birthday!), my mom brought out a box from the garage. It was wrapped in paper I recognized from last year. And, like last year, I made sure not to rip it when I opened it.

Underneath the wrapping paper was a shoebox.

I anxiously lifted the lid. Inside there were three items. A small container marked "FRAGILE," an envelope, and a flat, rectangular box.

I began with the fragile one because I already knew what it was.

It was a potato chip set on top of a couple tissues.

"So." My dad's eyes twinkled. "What is it?"

Dad worked in an artisanal potato chip factory. According to him, "artisanal" meant their stuff tastes better because they don't rely on machines as much. "The old-fashioned way," he'd say with pride. To me, "artisanal" meant "doing a lot of stuff by hand that machines could do." It also meant "expensive." *We* would never spend that much money on a bag of chips!

The company isn't very big, so my dad has a lot of different responsibilities, including creating new flavors and sorting the good chips from the bad. For every birthday, he brought me the most interesting discarded chip of the year. Then we played this game where I tried to guess what (or who!) the chip resembled.

I didn't have the heart to tell him that it felt like a little kid's game to me now.

I took the chip out of the box and held it up in front of me. It was kind of shriveled, and it seemed like it had . . . a beak?

"Is it a duck?"

"Not a duck!" My dad smiled.

I flipped it over. Maybe it wasn't a beak, but a wheel. "A tractor?"

"No!"

I rotated it ninety degrees and suddenly it looked less like a beak than a nose. And it had an expression on what definitely seemed like the face of . . . "The president?"

"Pin pon pin pon!" Dad made the sound they use on Japanese game shows for correct answers.

I smiled back at him. The reason I continued to humor my dad was because he usually looked like he'd been run over by a truck called life. Just this past year I noticed the area under his eyes looking darker and the skin sagging too. But not on my birthday. Not when we play this guessing game. His eyes crinkle and light up, and he looks a few years younger, even with his graying and thinning hair.

He carefully set the president potato chip in a square display case where he kept all the other ones he'd collected over the years. He opened the glass lid with a *creeeaaak* and placed it next to one that he calls Jun.

"Looks just like an old friend of mine," Dad explained when he'd brought that particular chip home years ago. It wasn't for my birthday or any special occasion, which was unusual for him. I took the chip from him and turned it this way and that. When I finally saw what he saw, I almost dropped it. Because the face in that chip looked trapped and frightened. Tormented, even.

"Yikes!" I squeaked. "Why would you keep this, Daddy? It's creepy!"

"The real Jun wasn't always like this," Dad told me. "Only toward the end." Then his eyes turned sad, and he looked out the window distractedly. Like he wasn't seeing the full moon that lit up our sky.

But then my mom burst into the room and announced,

"The rabbit in the moon is quite bright tonight!"

To which I answered, "You mean the 'man in the moon'?"

My mom sighed loudly. "You really can't see the rabbit in the moon? In Japan, we see a rabbit, not a man!"

"Well, maybe things are different here," I retorted.

"Yes, they certainly are!" My dad jumped in before my mom could scold me for my "attitude." He glanced over at my mom's skeptical face and added in a sunshiny-bright tone, "Exactly like we hoped they would be."

"Not *exactly.* . . ." My mom's response was more like a dark storm cloud gathering on the horizon. Even though I was only seven then, I knew there were a lot of things about "American" life that she didn't care for.

"Well, at least there's no Amanjaku." My dad crossed his arms.

My mom made a loud and sharp "*Ch!*" sound, like lightning striking the ground. That stopped Dad from saying anything more. "She's too young," she added.

Sure, I was little, but she didn't need to talk about me like I wasn't even there.

Aman-what? I wanted to ask my dad more. More about *why* he wanted things to be different. What were things like in Japan for him?

"Uriko." My mom pulled me from my memories by using the name I had shed years ago. She shook my next present at me. "Don't you want to open the rest? Because I can take this one back if you don't."

"I want to!" I responded, a bit louder than I meant to, and snatched the envelope from her hand.

Then her left eyebrow shot up, which was usually the signal that I was about to get a talking-to. But it was my birthday, so I could tell she was wavering about whether or not she should say anything.

Taking advantage of her hesitation, I rushed to open my card, even though I knew exactly what it would be.

"Twenty-four dollars! Double your age," my mom pointed out. "I can even take you shopping soon, if you like."

I nodded, relieved to see her eyebrow had settled back down. Twenty-four dollars could actually buy me a couple outfits at the Red, White, and Blue Thrift Store. But I might need to save it in case the final present wasn't what I wished for when I blew out the candles.

The box was the right size. I turned it this way and that. I rested it in my palm, trying to figure out if it was heavy enough to be the item I wanted more than anything. It was light, maybe too much so. The new ones were like that, though, right? I had to know for sure. I meant to be careful, but I couldn't help it—I ripped right through the wrapping paper to open this last one.

Only to find several scrunchies, each one a different color and pattern. I definitely needed them for my wild, hard-to-control hair, but . . .

It was not a phone. A phone like everyone at school had. A phone with a nice camera. A phone that wasn't embarrassing, like the one my parents gave me two years ago so they could reach me no matter where I was, but they controlled who I could call or text. A phone that would open up the world a little more for me.

"Do you like your presents?" My mom's question interrupted the daydream of what it would have been like to have my wish come true.

My parents' hopeful faces waited for my response.

"Thank you very much," I told them, like the good girl they expected me to be. *Like the good girl I want to be,* I thought as I tried to feel grateful instead of disappointed. A delicious, sort-of-homemade cake, some money, a funny gift from my dad, and pretty scrunchies were a lot more than some kids received for their birthday, I know. But it was hard not to compare myself to the kids at school who got even more. Kids who didn't celebrate their birthdays in a quiet, old house with no friends or siblings, just their two old parents on a Tuesday evening.

Since my birthday wish didn't come true, I wondered if I could change it. Not that I really believed in those types of things any more than I believed that I was born from a melon.

And just like that, my birthday was over. I knew it was when my mom asked me in her sweetest voice, "Melony-chan, are you sure you don't want to practice your piccolo?"

A good girl would have thought, *Look at the effort my parents put into my birthday!* A good girl would have responded,

"Of course, Mom! Thanks for the reminder."

But instead I thought, *It's my* birthday. *Who makes their kid practice their music on their birthday?* So, I answered (also in my sweetest voice), "I thought we agreed I could skip on my birthday and Christmas."

I almost regretted my response when disappointment flashed across my mom's face. But then she nodded. "Sou datta ne."

My dad agreed. "That's right! And you can just do more tomorrow, right?"

Something simmered and growled deep inside me then. Not the cake in my stomach. I'm not exactly sure what it was. But it poked, gurgled, grew louder, and it sounded a lot like "No!"

I squashed it, though—whatever it was—and just said, "Sure."

Late that night after both parents had gone to bed and I could hear their rumbling snores, I tiptoed down the hall. The bright moon cast an unearthly glow into our living room, directly onto my father's potato chip display. Perhaps it was a trick of the lighting, but the chip that resembled my father's friend almost seemed to . . . watch me. I stepped forward to inspect it and prove to myself how silly I was being but almost jumped out of my skin when an owl hooted loudly outside. "Whoo! Whoo, whoo, who?" as if demanding to know who was intruding in its night domain.

I quickly made my way into the kitchen and rummaged through the drawer where we kept the matches and lit one.

It flared up and brightened the small corner near the sink where I stood.

What should I wish for? As the flame grew and traveled down the matchstick, I realized I should have thought this through *before* lighting it.

Something different, I thought. *Adventure.* The light—and heat—danced closer to my fingers.

Freedom.

At that moment the wind picked up and whistled through the trees. *At what cost? What cossst?* it seemed to whisper.

Any, I answered in my mind. Impulsively, without *really* considering what that meant.

At this last wish, I blew out the match.

Little did I know that my wish would come true—or that it would endanger everything and everyone I held dear.

But more on that later.

Chapter TWO

"E ur . . . Eureka . . . Eureka Yoshimura?" The substitute band teacher, unsurprisingly, botched my name the next day during fifth period.

"Urine Girl," snickered Hunter, a boy I'd known for years.

"Pssssss." His buddy Jay made the sound of pee.

These boys have been thorns in my side since kindergarten. I call them "Miasma" and "Scat" because "miasma" is a poisonous cloud that lingers in the air—like after someone farts—and "scat" is just a fancy word for wild animal poo, and these terms describe them perfectly. Plus, Hunter and Jay don't know what the words mean, and they can't be bothered to look them up. Technically, they're not bad words, either, so I can't get in trouble for using them.

My real name, the Japanese one my parents gave me, is Uriko, and it's the one that appears on the attendance sheet. Teachers almost always seem relieved at the beginning of each year when I tell them to call me Melony instead, even though Uriko is pretty easy to pronounce—"oo-ree-ko."

My name means "child of an uri." But early on, a girl named Ashleigh figured out that it also started with the same three letters as the word "urine." I had barely started school at the time, but I still knew that a nickname of Pee-Pee Girl would make life real hard for me, so I threw a fit and told my parents I wouldn't return unless they let me change my name.

"But Uriko is who you are!" they insisted. So they sent me back to school, but I got into "accidents" with whoever teased me.

First, I "accidentally" knocked a carton of milk into Hunter's lap.

Then I "mistakenly" kicked Jay's shin instead of the soccer ball during recess. "Oops," I told him. "I slipped."

But when I pulled out Ashleigh's big red hair bow and stomped on it, it was kinda difficult to convince anyone that I didn't actually mean to do that (plus, there were witnesses). My kindergarten teacher called my parents to school to have a meeting that the principal attended too.

Even though I explained exactly why I acted the way I did, everyone in charge made it crystal clear that *I* was going to have to change my behavior.

"Think of how Ashleigh must feel," the principal said.

Think of how it feels to be called Pee-Pee Girl, I thought. But I couldn't say that because they'd just turn it around on me.

But my mom and dad looked shaken and pale after that

meeting—so much so that I *did* feel sorry. Not for the kids I got into scuffles with, but for disappointing my parents, which made me feel like a shriveled-up raisin left under a sofa collecting dust. So I promised them that I would behave from now on as long as no one teased me. And I convinced them that if I wasn't Uriko anymore, then no one would.

My parents wanted me to keep my new name as close to my real one as possible, though. Something about "not losing sight of where you come from." So we looked at names like Ursula and Oona, even Eureka. But I didn't like any of them.

"Why does it have to sound like Uriko?" I remember asking at the time.

"Maybe we can translate it instead?" Mom suggested as she brought out our very large, well-used Japanese-English dictionary and looked it up. "Uri" had two definitions: melon *and* gourd.

"You would rather be Melon Child instead of Uriko?" my mom asked.

"You could also be Gourd Kid," my dad pointed out.

Of course I didn't want my new name to be Melon Child or Gourd Kid.

"I know that Gordon is a name," my father mused. "And I've heard the name Melanie before, so why not Melony? You know, like 'melon' with a *Y*?"

"I like Gordon!" was my mom's response to Dad's suggestion.

"Isn't that a boy's name?" I asked.

"Well then, how about Gordanna? Or Gordy? Gordita?" my dad brainstormed.

I was pretty sure that a "gordita" was something sold at the Mexican food restaurant nearby. Not that my parents ever took me there, but I saw it on TV once.

"I like Melony," I decided.

"That's . . . fine," my parents agreed, although they didn't sound too thrilled about it. "But Melony must be a good girl, do you understand?"

I nodded. And at the time, I fully intended to try my best!

"Eureka?" the teacher called out again.

I didn't answer. I knew she *meant* "Uriko," but something inside me refused to respond to her today. Nobody pointed out who I was, either. Miasma and Scat were sitting in the wrong seats and had switched instruments with each other. Typical behavior for a lot of my classmates when our band instructor, Ms. Delgado, was absent, although I didn't really mind because it meant Miasma wouldn't be in the piccolo section with me. Even though he played better than I did, I was glad to be relieved of his super-annoying presence.

Ppppbltltlt. Miasma honked on Scat's tuba as his sidekick cackled alongside him.

With a few clicks on the keyboard, the sub sent the attendance report to the front office.

"Okay, class, uh . . ." The teacher read the instructions that Ms. Delgado had left for her as she handed out packets of paper. "Apparently there's going to be a three-day, two-night band trip this spring to the Sunshine Fun Center and Amusement Park in which the whole band will be invited to play in their spring break concert. The cost is quite reasonable and there will be several fundraising opportunities to help out. Tryouts will also be held a few months ahead of time for a smaller, exclusive ensemble that will compete with other selected groups. Plus, if you make that group, you'll go for free!"

Technically, our school had an "away for the day" cell phone policy, but since our regular teacher was *also* away, lots of kids brought their devices out of their pockets to play. Games, funny videos, pictures of cute pets—everyone had a window to the outside world . . . except me. So, I actually paid attention. A trip? A three-day *overnight* trip?

"Ms. Delgado will discuss this more when she returns. But for right now, she'd like you to talk about it with your parents. There will be an informational session in a few weeks. . . ."

I scanned through the handout. A flight to California. Time to enjoy the amusement park, free time at the beach.

There was *no way* my mom and dad would agree to this, but . . .

I tucked the forms into my binder.

My next class was also intriguing but decidedly more productive. For one, our English teacher, Mr. Sutton, *made* it that way. His hair and neatly trimmed beard were all white, and he wore a dress shirt and tie every day. He didn't put up with kids who goofed off, and he always challenged us with our writing. We knew a first draft was never the last one, and we groaned when we saw all his corrections and comments—all made with his fancy fountain pen that he kept in a special case when he wasn't using it.

I know he doesn't sound like a typical favorite teacher, but he was mine.

Mr. Sutton wasn't the only reason I liked this class. Another reason was because the most velvety floppy-eared bunny I'd ever held lived there. He was named the Dread Pirate R because he was white with black spots, mostly on his right side, and one big patch over his left eye. Plus, *R* stood for "rabbit," and we also named him on Talk Like a Pirate Day (which happens to be September 19, if you'd like to mark it on your calendar). So, it was extra fun to be able to say his name like "the Dread Pirate Arrrrrrrrrrr!"

Whenever class became boring (which wasn't that often, but even Mr. Sutton had his off days), I'd just watch the Dread Pirate R take two hops across his cage, sip from his water bottle, and then—*hop, hop*—back to the other side again. There were pets in several of my elementary school classes, but Mr. Sutton was the only middle school teacher who had one. Apparently, he inherited Sir Fluffy-Floppy-Cutie-Patootie from Mrs. Morris, the science teacher who retired last year. I liked that he didn't try to get rid of him and that he let us give him a *much* more dignified name. Even though Hunter—I mean, Miasma—had snorted, "Bunnies are for babies!" on the first day of school, I saw him and his buddy Scat watching the Dread Pirate R just as much as I did.

But Mr. Sutton and the Dread Pirate R weren't the reasons why class was different today. It was different because there was a new girl.

And she looked like me. Well, kind of.

We were about the same height, but she was pale and nervous. She stood next to Mr. Sutton playing with the ends of her stick-straight hair. My hair was thick and wavy and kinked every which way when I didn't have it pulled back in a braid. But hers was the same deep black as mine, and her eyes were also a dark, warm brown.

"Attention, everyone!" Mr. Sutton raised his hand and gazed sternly at everyone through his gold-rimmed glasses. The room quieted at once.

"Chloë Yoshida will be joining our class. She just moved here from California, so I'd like you all to be as helpful and kind as I know you are."

Yoshida? Even our last names were similar.

"Melony?" Mr. Sutton pointed Chloë toward the empty desk next to mine. It was where my best friend, Louisa, used to sit. That is—before she left. "I'd like you to help Chloë this week, all right? You have pretty much the same schedule."

Really? She wasn't in any of my classes this morning. Chloë shuffled as quickly as she could toward her new seat.

"My mom let me sleep in," she whispered, as if she heard what I was thinking. "I wish she hadn't. Now I'll still be the new kid tomorrow morning too."

"All right, everyone use the next ten minutes to gather the materials for your research report." Mr. Sutton sure didn't waste any class time.

"Okay, well, you should get your notebook out. . . ." I mumbled to the new girl as I scrambled to fish mine out from my backpack. My locker was on a different floor from all my classes, so I had to stuff my bag full with everything I needed for the day. It was as heavy as a boulder!

Turns out Chloë was already on the ball. She opened a notebook and wrote "Research Report" at the top with a sharp new pencil and "Chloë Yoshida" in clear, neat letters underneath.

I couldn't help but notice her *perfect* handwriting and the slow, deliberate way she circled in the two dots over the *E* in her name.

"It's an umlaut," Chloë told me without looking up.

"Huh." I couldn't tell if I was annoyed she answered a question that I didn't ask or impressed she knew what I was thinking.

Mr. Sutton walked by and handed Chloë the directions for the report. He had written her name on the sheet already, complete with the two dots over the *E*. Chloë nodded approvingly.

"There are two types of people," Chloë said to me as she read the paper. "Those who respect the umlaut and those who don't."

"Oh yeah?" This new kid was kinda weird, but I was intrigued by where our conversation was going. "What if they don't use it and just write a regular *E*?"

"Then we couldn't be friends," she responded matter-of-factly.

I nodded. There were those who spelled my name "Melony" and those who spelled it "Melanie" and continued to do so even after I'd corrected them. I totally got where Chloë was coming from.

"So, we can write about *anything*?" Chloë's brow furrowed when she finished reading the directions for the report.

"Pretty much." I shrugged. "But you have to get your topic approved first. I'm writing mine on owls," I offered.

"Owls, huh?" Chloë looked thoughtful. "Interesting. Have you ever seen a nutria? I saw one for the first time and I thought it was—"

"Melony Yoshimura?" A voice from the door to the classroom interrupted Chloë before she could complete her thought. It was Ms. Jain, a woman from the front office, and . . . my *mom*.

Mom's eyes looked wild as she scanned the classroom. When she spotted me, she rushed over, Japanese words tumbling from her mouth.

"The office called me and said you weren't in your last

class. You scared me half to death!"

I squirmed in my seat. "Mama, shinpai shinakutemo ii yo. Zuutto koko ni itan da yo!" But then I felt all my classmates' eyes on me.

"Naruto arigato!" I heard Jay (aka Scat) whisper the only Japanese words he knew to Hunter.

"Sukiyaki ichiro konichiwa," Hunter (aka Miasma) responded in garbled Japanese, but *not* in a whisper. Everyone giggled. Everyone except for Chloë and Mr. Sutton, who silenced them with a piercing look.

I switched to English. "Don't worry—I've been here the whole time, Mom."

I don't know why I felt the need to translate for the kids who were listening in. But I did it anyway.

Ms. Jain nodded to Mr. Sutton. "I'm sure it was just the sub's mistake with the attendance form from last period. Melony's not the type to skip out."

"No, she definitely isn't." Mr. Sutton nodded.

Then Ms. Jain opened the door, but my mom stayed glued next to me.

"Mom," I muttered. "I'm in class."

Mom nodded, her panic seeming to subside. But she wouldn't move.

My mom didn't look like my classmates' moms. When other moms needed to stop by the school, they were either easy and breezy like they had just stepped out of a salon or frazzled in pajama bottoms or sweatpants with some sort of stain on their shirts. My mom was neither. She was always neat, but not flashy, with her gray hair trimmed short over the ears. She looked so much older, as old as Mr. Sutton, in fact. It wasn't that I was embarrassed by my mother, but I also didn't like how everyone was staring at her. At us.

Mr. Sutton approached. "If you like, you're welcome to take her home early. It's last period. We're just working on some writing for the rest of the class, and Melony knows what to do."

My mom nodded again, relieved. I wish my parents would just let me ride the bus home like all the other kids, but no.

"Nothing good happens on the bus," they told me when I started school many years ago. And so, without fail, either my mom or dad had picked me up or dropped me off to and from school every single day.

My cheeks burned as I stuffed everything in my backpack, and I felt Chloë's eyes on us when we walked out the door.

dropped everything off in my room after we arrived home from school. Then I went to the bathroom and splashed cold water on my face, like I could wash off the embarrassment of my mom busting into Mr. Sutton's class. Or was it anger that I felt bubbling up inside me? I pushed it down. After all, if I blew up, there was no way she'd consider letting me go on that overnight band trip.

Mom means well, I also told myself. *She was just worried.*

But why? Our little town was voted the second safest place to live in Oregon. The number one place literally has twenty-three people living there, so that's the only reason we're number two. There are barely any robberies or break-ins, so people call the police to complain about dogs barking too loudly or the weeds growing too tall behind the local grocery store. Nothing happens here. *Nothing.*

By the time I came out to grab a snack, Mom was at the dining room table, working on her quilt like nothing out of the ordinary had happened today. I recognized some of the patterns that she must have used to make my birthday scrunchies.

Like I often did when Mom was engrossed in her quilting, I began preparing her a cup of tea. First, I found her favorite teacup—ivory, with splashes of teal—scooped barely a teaspoon of green tea leaves into a small orange clay teapot, and then used our hot water dispenser to fill it. I waited two minutes, then poured the tea, making sure to leave plenty of room at the top so it wasn't "nami nami," or filled to the brim and about to spill. She didn't look up as I set it on a wooden coaster in front of her, on top of the plastic sheet that protected a hand-painted tablecloth that covered our dark mahogany table. Mom did most of her quilting in our formal dining room, which was where we would eat when we had guests over. Since we never did, though, it became mom's quilting room instead.

Mom always seemed to relax when she had her tea. She didn't seem mad, though, over what happened at school. She was already deep into the details of her handiwork. To earn extra money, my mom was a tailor. It mostly involved hemming pants and dresses, fixing broken zippers, even simple stuff like replacing a lost button. She was really meticulous, so she had steady work, but she was happiest when she could spend time on her own projects. Mom liked to hand-piece as much of her quilts as possible, so it had taken the two of us close to a year to put this one together.

"Come look here." Mom pointed at the patch she had been working on. "This is the backyard of the house I grew up in. It wasn't very big, but there was a Momiji that turned so red! Bloodred, in fact."

Geez, Mom. Kind of a gross comparison, I thought.

I watched as Mom's finger traced the delicate stitches outlining what seemed like every detail of the tree. There was a Momiji—a Japanese maple—in our yard here in Oregon too. Its deep crimson leaves hung on to their branches and the dewy raindrops dangled off the leaves. When the sun caught them just right, *I* always thought they sparkled like rubies, not drops of blood.

But Mom was too lost in her memories of her Japanese backyard to think of everything we had now. "There were sliding doors here, and this is where the loom was set up. I wish we could have brought it, but it was simply too much trouble to try to ship. It had been in our family for generations, you know." She sang in a wistful low voice:

*"Pata pata pat-tan, tat-ton ton
Pata pata pat-tan, tat-ton ton.*

"Those are the sounds it would make as I passed the threads back and forth. Switched the pedals, right, then left. I wish you could see some of the fabrics I wove. One roll of fabric could take a year, but they were one of a kind and so soft. Nothing like these stiff, machine-made cloths. If only

I could have taught you, too, like your grandmother taught me."

I always felt bad for my mom when she talked about my grandmother, who died before I could ever meet her, and was missing her loom. Quilting was clearly just a substitute for it—even so, she was able to piece together amazingly detailed scenes with scraps of fabric most people would have just thrown away.

There was a new patch today. On it was something that looked like Grover from *Sesame Street*, only it was gray and hiding behind the cloth flower Mom had placed on the square.

"What's that?" I pointed to it.

Mom took so long in answering that I thought maybe she didn't hear me.

"Since you're twelve now, it's time you knew," she finally replied. "This is the Amanjaku, and it's the reason why your father wanted to leave Japan."

Amanjaku, Amanjaku. I've heard this word before, but when? Then I remembered the creepy potato chip that Dad had said looked like his old friend Jun. And how when I tried to ask more about it, my mom had stopped him because she said I was "too young." I was excited that I was finally, *finally* old enough to know.

I'd always wondered why my parents were here in Oregon, so far from where they grew up and where I was born. When I'd asked before, Mom had explained, "Your great-uncle said he'd sponsor us, so we thought it would be a nice opportunity to see the world."

I never believed that explanation, not for a second. For one, every so often, there would be a cryptic comment about things being different here, like the one my dad made when he talked about his sad-looking potato chip friend.

And the other thing was, my parents never got out to "see the world." Even when my class needed chaperones for cool field trips, like the ones where we got to release baby salmon into a river or go hiking through forests and caves, did they ever volunteer? Nope!

My dad was often at work in the factory, but my mom's schedule was flexible. She could have come along, but she preferred to hear my stories later, about how the baby fish were able to swim away before the ospreys could scoop them up, or how my arms turned bumpy like chicken skin when I ventured through chilly caverns as dark as night.

I wondered if this "Amanjaku" had anything to do with why my parents—my mom, especially—always seemed so fearful of "the outside."

But the creature on the quilt didn't look scary at all. It resembled a harmless fuzzy Muppet, in my opinion.

"What's an 'amanjaku'?" I asked. "Is it an animal?"

"Not exactly. More like an evil spirit. A demon, maybe? I don't know the English word for it because it's Japanese. There aren't any here."

For some reason, I felt disappointed when my mom told

me this. Even though she called it evil, it just looked lonely to me. Lonely like I was ever since graduating from elementary, having my best friend move, and my other friends attend the other middle school. Lonely like I was as an only child—

"The Amanjaku had come to your father's village," Mom continued as she stitched the flower into place. "You might remember your father mentioning his friend Jun years ago, right? The Amanjaku preys on children—usually elementary school–aged—before they enter middle school and become more responsible. The Amanjaku is the thing that convinced Jun to behave horribly. So much so that he brought a great deal of suffering on his family and community. We didn't want that to happen to you."

I couldn't help it, but I let out an exasperated sigh. Even though this was more interesting than my melon origin story, all this nonsense about the Amanjaku seemed like just another one of those tales—a made-up baby story, for what purpose? So I'd be scared into *not* behaving horribly? Did my parents really think I believed in evil spirits and demons and that I came from a melon?

All of a sudden, the air in the house felt heavy, like it was closing in on me, and I couldn't breathe. I had to get out. Walk in the woods behind the house. Forage for the oyster mushrooms that grow by the creek. Try to locate the barred owls whose distinctive hoots sound like they're asking, "Who cooks for you? Who cooks for y'aalllll?" Anything. *Anything* for a bit of freedom.

"Mother?" I stood up and asked in as sweet a tone as I could muster. "May I go outside now, please?"

My mom looked out the window and took in the sun that created a bright square of light on the quilt. She squinted and stared into the distance as if searching for something, as if she didn't trust the clear skies.

"You'll wear a jacket? It looks cold."

"Sure."

"And stay where I can see you?"

Unbelievable! She just said that there wasn't an Amanjaku here, that they left it behind in Japan. So why was my mom still fearful of everything? My old friend Louisa's mom let her bike everywhere by herself. To the store, to school. I was *twelve* now, and in middle school. Not like a baby fifth grader. At least my parents let me go places with Louisa. "Safety in numbers," Mom would sometimes say to herself as we headed out the door. But now that my friend had left, it looked like I wasn't going to be going *anywhere* anymore.

Then a realization struck me. Maybe these were just excuses. Maybe the times they'd let me have some freedom were the exception rather than the rule. Maybe their reasons would change, but my situation would always remain the same. *Protected* in their minds, but *controlled* in mine.

"There are other things to fear here." My mom confirmed my thoughts as she focused on the quilt. "It's not that I don't trust you; I don't trust him," she explained as she nodded to the window facing our front lawn.

Just then a scruffy-looking elderly man shuffled on the sidewalk in front of our house, almost like he had been summoned. It was the man whose backyard bumped up to ours. I think, anyway. It seemed like him and it also didn't. We didn't know our neighbors well because we've always kept to ourselves, mostly.

Almost as if he knew I was watching him, he turned and seemed to peer right into our window. When our eyes locked, icicles shot through my veins. How was it even possible he could see me from where he was standing? He did, though, I swear—and my body locked and froze in response. But then his gaze turned back to the street, and I shook off the feeling of dread, sure that I had imagined it. He was never particularly friendly when I'd bumped into him before, and my parents had always said, "Stranger danger!" when I tried to talk to him when I was little. But they said that about a lot of people, and for some reason today felt . . . different.

Did Mom just see the same thing I did? I wondered. *Or did she somehow summon him to make her point?*

I didn't like how Mom was trying to rub her worries off on me. I slumped down into the seat next to her. *How can I convince her to let me go on a field trip to another state if this is how she acts when I want to go outside?* I thought. *I sure hope the matchstick wish comes true.* I closed my eyes and pleaded to the universe, *Pleasepleasepleaseplease.*

But when I opened my eyes, there were no signs that anything had changed. That anything would *ever* change.

"Fine, I'll just stay inside," I muttered.

"Ooh, I have an idea!" My mom's face brightened. "You could practice your piccolo while I work. I love listening to your music."

That was the *last* thing I wanted to do.

But my mom took a sip of the tea I had brought her, smiled like we had agreed on something, and returned to her quilting.

I stomped off to my room and threw my sheet music onto my flimsy metal stand with a clatter. As I was about to blow on my piccolo as loudly as I could to hurt Mom's ears, I stopped. *What if I played well?* a voice inside me whispered. After all, that could help convince my parents to let me go on the band trip. There's no way they'd agree at this moment, but if I worked on them over time, then . . . maybe? So, I played and played until I felt dizzy as I tried to ignore the sunny sky and gentle breeze that beckoned, *Come outside, come outside.*

Not yet, I thought. *But soon.*

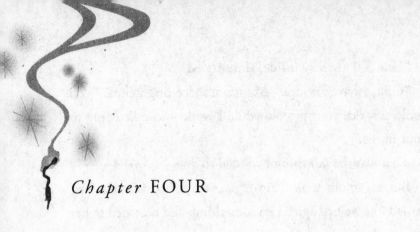

Chapter FOUR

You would think that all kids like recess, but we don't. Especially those of us who don't have any friends, like me. I wanted to spend the time in the library getting lost in the adventures only a book could provide. But during our first parent-teacher conference, my homeroom teacher snitched on me. When he mentioned it might be healthier for me to go outside and get some exercise and fresh air, my mom nodded in agreement. Especially after she was able to confirm there were recess aides to watch over all of us.

I thought it was very controlling of Mom to try to dictate what I did at school as well as home. But I didn't want to argue, so I always took a book out to the playground to read. I knew Mom wanted me to move around some, too, but I didn't feel like walking around and around the track like some of the kids did, going nowhere. There were also some kids who pretended they were ninja cats as they clambered up the jungle gym. One day when I'd gone closer to check them out, they hissed at me and darted away. No big deal because I wasn't *really* all that interested.

There was another group that stood around and did nothing. Girls and boys together, looking at their phones, taking selfies. I guess they thought they were being cool, but in my opinion, it was more like *cold*, because that's how they acted toward anyone who wasn't already part of their arctic circle. On frosty October days, all the girls wore the same cozy, warm beige boots. I didn't particularly envy them as people, but their fleece-lined footwear . . . that's a different story. I told myself they needed them more than me, though. To warm up their toes through which ice-cold blood flowed, I imagined.

I didn't fit in with any of these kids or options. A year ago, in fifth grade, I had the perfect little four-person friend group. But Louisa was the glue that held us together. When it came time for the kids at Oak River Elementary to choose which middle school to go to, Sophia and Olivia chose Cedar Ridge and I got stuck here at Rosecreek Middle School.

"Cedar Ridge has a better choir program." Sophia justified her decision.

"My brother is already there," explained Olivia.

When I asked my parents about the possibility of going to the same middle school, too, Mom responded, "Cedar Ridge? That's fifteen minutes farther away. You can go to Rosecreek with Louisa."

"But she's moving, remember?" A desperate whine crept into my voice. "Please? I could ride the bus."

But we all knew what they thought of the bus.

So, the day after I refused to answer to "Eureka" and my mom stormed my English class, I prepared to sit down with a book I'd checked out from the library in my regular hiding place—the concrete steps that led down to the far end of the track—when I saw the new girl Chloë was already there.

At first I didn't know how to feel. Annoyed? But she noticed me right away and scooted over to make room.

"Oh, hi there!" She greeted me almost like *I* was the new kid. "Is this your spot? I can move if you want."

But as she waited for me to answer, the look of desperation in her eyes was unmistakable. I felt sorry for her. Even though I didn't have much in common with a lot of my classmates in middle school, at least I was aware of that. For Chloë, it would be trial and error until she found someone decent to hang out with. That is, unless . . .

"You're fine," I let her know as I sat next to her. Then I noticed the book that *she* was holding. It was open to a blank page. "What's that?" I asked.

"Oh." Chloë looked embarrassed. "It's just a notebook. My best friend gave it to me. It's from France."

So Chloë had a best friend, too, who left. Or maybe she was the one who left by moving up here.

Chloë paused as if she was debating whether she should tell me something. She closed the notebook and leaned over as if to protect it. She took a deep breath. "I write things sometimes. Or draw. More like doodle. They're not all that good." And then she looked terrified, like she was afraid I'd actually ask to *see* some of her work.

The interesting thing about middle school was that there were so many more kids here than at our elementary school. So, in some ways we could be different from who we were last year. We went from classroom to classroom, and, sure, a few of the same kids were in each class, but a lot of the time there was a whole new mix of students each period. After Louisa left, I was too sad to try to make new friends. In elementary school, there were "friendship benches" you could sit on at recess if you wanted to find someone to play with, but there weren't any here. I'm not sure anybody would have used them even if there were! The vibe in middle school was way different—announcing to the world that you didn't have someone to hang out with wouldn't go over so well, to say the least.

But maybe making a new friend here on the steps by the track would be all right.

"You write?" I asked. "That's perfect. I read!" I showed her my book.

Chloë smiled, and it seemed like it was out of relief. "Cool! What's it about?"

"I don't know." I shrugged. "I just brought it out here for something to do."

Chloë laughed. "Same!"

"I used to go to the library for lunch, but my mom heard about it and insisted—"

"You get some fresh air and exercise?" Chloë finished for me.

"Yeah! How'd you know?"

"My mom says the exact same thing. She says it will help with 'my mood.'" Chloë emphasized these last two words with air quotes.

Both of us laughed, even as I wondered to myself why Chloë needed to improve her mood at all. She seemed pretty cheerful to me! I was about to ask when Chloë stood up.

"Do you wanna walk?" she asked. "I'm getting chilly."

I didn't really feel like it, not only because the day felt warm to me, but also because a little part of me didn't want to end up doing exactly what our mothers wanted us to do. But Chloë *had* just moved here from sunny California, and she was starting to shiver.

I got up. "Sure!"

"But you should tie your shoe first." Chloë pointed at my unraveled laces. "Wouldn't want you to trip!"

"Oh, thanks." I bent down to double-knot my bow. *That was nice of her*, I thought.

So, neither of us ended up reading or writing, but we joined the rest of the sixth graders on the track. When I'd watched my classmates plod around and around the oval before, they reminded me of a book I'd picked up once at the library. My mom was taking so long leafing through the crafting and quilting books that before I knew it, I found myself browsing outside the kids' section and reading a story about a guy in prison and how the most exciting part of his day was when he and his buddies were let out into the jail yard to amble about for their daily exercise. Just like us, they weren't allowed beyond the tall fence that surrounded the grounds. But when I stepped onto the track with Chloë today, I didn't feel as much like a prisoner as I thought I would.

Mile after mile we walked that week. And we talked.

"Do your parents speak Japanese?" I asked Chloë.

"No. But I think my dad's grandparents did. A little," Chloë answered. "It's cool that you can speak it with your mom. I wish I could speak Japanese."

I remembered how I stuck out like a sore thumb when my mom burst into our class, shouting at me in Japanese. I never thought that some kids would think it was cool. For some reason, this made me feel taller all of a sudden. That is, until we walked past Miasma and Scat.

"Hey, did you know that Weedle evolves into Kakuna?" Miasma yelled.

Chloë slowed down. "Is he asking me?"

"Just keep walking," I said as I tried to make it obvious we were ignoring them.

"That's a pretty random thing to ask." Chloë side-eyed them as we approached.

"They're assuming because we look Japanese that we like Pokémon," I explained.

"That's a pretty random thing to assume," Chloë responded.

I looked straight ahead and kept on striding past Miasma and his ever-present sidekick, Scat. "I guess some people have their own ideas and try to make everyone fit inside them."

I was talking about those two twerps when I said that, but then I realized they weren't the only ones trying to make others fit their idea of what they should be. Just like we were trudging around the track over and over, my mind swirled around something Ms. Jain said the other day: "Melony's not the type to skip class," and how Mr. Sutton had replied, "No, she definitely isn't."

How do they *know?* a little voice inside me whispered.

My mind circled even farther back to when I changed from Uriko to Melony just so kids would stop teasing me. I pondered the bargain I had made with my parents then when they said, "But Melony must be a good girl."

I didn't question them one bit all those years ago, but at the memory, the little voice spoke again, and louder:

Why?

Then a question from Chloë pulled me from my spiraling thoughts.

"Hey, I told my parents about you, and they want to meet you! Want to come over to my place on Friday night?"

Chapter FIVE

Just like I had yet to ask my parents about the overnight band trip, I waited to ask my parents about going over to Chloë's.

You see, they've always been weird about letting me hang out at other people's places. At first I thought this was how all parents were, you know, in this day and age with how the world is and all, but I quickly learned that my mom and dad were also what a lot of people call "helicopter parents." My parents grew up in small towns where everyone knew everyone, or at least had heard about everyone else. Things were different here in the US, and my mom was especially suspicious.

We used to play this game called What If . . .

"What if a stranger asked you to help find his puppy?" my mom would ask.

"I wouldn't! He's probably trying to kidnap me!" I answered.

"What if a van—"

"Without windows?"

"With *or* without windows—pulled up next to you and asked if you wanted candy?"

"Run and call the police!"

"What if you get lost in a crowd?"

"Find someone who looks like a mama to help me!"

I know that all that seems pretty reasonable. But then the game would get even more specific.

"What if someone came to school to drive you home because they said I asked them to?"

"Well, if you asked them to, then I guess that would be oka—"

"No!" my mom corrected me at the time. "I would call the office and let them know something like that."

"Oh." I was surprised, but that made sense. "Okay. But what if there's a power outage and Wi-Fi goes down and cell phones stop working?"

My dad nodded. "We should definitely run through a list of people we'd trust to drive you home."

That didn't take very long, though. They basically said my teacher at the time—Mrs. Sawyer—and Louisa's parents were fine. No one else.

Now, since Louisa had moved and it had been years since I was in Mrs. Sawyer's class, those people weren't options anymore.

So when I arrived home that day, I washed my face and

hands like I always did after being out and sat down to eat the carrot sticks my mom had prepared for a snack.

As I munched on them, I gazed outside at our backyard neighbor's persimmon tree. It hadn't shed its leaves yet, and the orange fruit my mom and I both loved was just beginning to ripen. Every year, I thought about using our rickety step-stool to climb over into the neighbor's yard and pick some of them. It wouldn't have been stealing, not really—otherwise, they were just left to rot on their lawn! I never took any, though, because my parents already said I couldn't.

"Please, can't we just see if we can have a few?" I asked when I was younger. But my mom only looked worried and said that the old man who lived there "isn't friendly."

As I crunched my carrot sticks, I imagined they were persimmons instead. After all, they were the same color . . . but persimmons were juicy, at least when they had ripened just so—a little bit like a peach, but firmer, and without any of the tart. These carrots were definitely *not* juicy.

"Whoo? Who?"

I stopped my snacking for a moment to listen. It had been a long time since I'd spotted an owl in our yard. The last one I saw I had named Bob, but that was years ago and in the evening. Since then, I've only heard them at night, not in the middle of the afternoon like today. I waited for it to hoot again, but the woods remained still and quiet except for the lonely *chirp*, *chirp* of a sparrow. *Maybe it was just a branch falling*, I convinced myself.

When I finished my last carrot, I took my plate to the sink and washed it, too. Mom didn't notice, though, since she'd been wrapped up in her quilting ever since I returned home. She was humming her weaving song softly to herself while she worked:

"Pata pata pat-tan, tat-ton ton.
Pata pata pat-tan, tat-ton ton."

As I was drying the plate and about to put it in the cabinet to the right of the sink, an owl flew into the window with a giant *KATHUNK!*

I shrieked and dropped the plate with a clatter.

"Melony, doushita no?" My mom rushed into the kitchen.

"I, uh—" It took me a moment to calm my pounding heart and find my words. "An owl. It hit the window—"

"An owl?" My mom looked out the window. "I don't see anything. Are you sure you didn't imagine it?"

I'm sure I hadn't. Not even the foreboding look it gave me as it disappeared into the woods.

"Californians? Hmm." My dad grunted as he dipped his spoon into the warm, thick, and spicy curry blanketed over pillowy, steaming rice. It was a simple dinner, but one of my favorites, and perfect for a cold autumn evening like this one. It was another long day at work for him, and I could tell he just wanted to sit and eat.

"That's what I said, too." Mom fished out extra carrots and onions from the pot of curry and added them to my plate. "I don't know about Californians." I liked my mom's curry, but I'd *just* had carrots for a snack earlier. *What does she think I am? A rabbit?* I wondered if the Dread Pirate R would like curried carrots as a change from the kibble and hay he ate, day in and day out.

"What about Louisa?" Dad asked.

"I told you, she's gone," I answered.

"Oh, that's right—their RV adventure." My dad nodded. "That Lyons family—such free spirits!"

"Hmm." My mom responded in a way that made it clear she approved of neither adventures nor free spirits.

And then—I don't know why, but—my lip started to quiver, and I could barely keep my voice from shaking. The sharp hurt of missing my friend had dulled into a slow ache over the past few weeks. Or so I had thought.

"Please? Chloë's very nice. I'm sure you could come in for the first few minutes and talk with her mom . . ."

My dad nodded as if that seemed like a reasonable idea. Mom, on the other hand . . . I could practically see her calculating the risk. *Would this happen in Japan? Maybe. Would a Japanese family invite me in to introduce themselves? Yes, absolutely. Would an American family? Uncertain result! Does not compute!*

"No, I don't think so. What if she doesn't invite me in?" With her response, my mom confirmed what she was thinking. "Then I'll be dropping you off at some strangers' place. Do you know anything about her family at all?"

I couldn't understand why my parents were making it so hard for me to make new friends. "Chloë's mom is a dentist and her dad works from home while he takes care of her and her older sister," I blurted out. "She said he plays the ukulele and they eat popcorn on Friday nights. They have a curly-tailed dog who hates baths and getting his nails trimmed. He looks like a fox and his ears go flat like the wings of an airplane when he's happy—"

But none of this information changed the look of skepticism on my parents' faces. That is, until I added, "And her last name's Yoshida."

Mom perked up immediately. "Yoshida?"

"They're Japanese?" Dad asked.

"Well . . ." I didn't know how to explain my friend to my parents. Before I met her, I hadn't realized there are actually all sorts of Japanese and the Yoshidas aren't exactly the same type of Japanese my parents are.

"Her dad's family came over to work in Hawaii a really long time ago. But her mom's mom is actually a Japanese Brazilian married to a Japanese American, but Chloë's mom grew up in California."

"Oh!" my parents said at the same time. I couldn't tell if it was a good "oh!" or a bad "oh!"

"They seem very interesting!" my dad said. "I should like to meet them."

"Do they speak Japanese?" my mom asked. I could sense my mom redoing her previous risk calculation based on this new information—*bee bee beep*, *bee beep*, *bee beep*.

"Umm . . ." I was so relieved they were excited that I didn't want to break the news that the Yoshidas only spoke English. But I couldn't lie. "Chloë says they took a few classes, but not really."

"Oh." My mom was clearly let down.

"Oh." My dad was too.

"But they wish they could!" I added with as much pep as I could muster. I hoped my enthusiasm would bring back some of theirs. "Oh please, please, oh please, may I go to Chloë's on Friday? Please?"

My parents traded looks and took a very long time to answer. Too long. With each second, clouds of disappointment threatened to dim any ray of hope that I'd been holding on to.

"No," my mother finally answered. "But she may come here. And please let her know that I would like to meet her parents if they'd like to stop in when they drop her off."

It wasn't quite a victory, but it was a step toward one. Part of me did worry how in the world I'd get them to agree to an overnight band trip if this was how much they resisted my simple request to go to a new friend's house. But the other part of me couldn't help but feel a glimmer of hope, like the flame from the match that had brightened the night of my birthday. Even if only for a second or two.

Chapter SIX

When Chloë came over to hang out on Friday, it felt as if she and her dad had studied the rule book *How to Impress the Hard-to-Please Yoshimuras*.

First of all, her hair was freshly brushed and she was wearing a different (clean) shirt than she wore at school. Then, she and her dad slipped off their shoes without being asked (another silent test my mom used to assess the character of our visitors).

"Hi, I'm George Yoshida!" Chloë's dad shook both my parents' hands vigorously. "Thank you so much for having Chloë over!"

Then he handed my mom a small semitransparent plastic bag full of bright orange fruit.

"Persimmons?" my mom asked excitedly before she peered into the bag.

"Well, no." Mr. Yoshida looked sheepish. "They're just clementines."

Now it was my mom's turn to feel awkward. "Oh, we love those, too."

"I get it, though." Chloë's dad nodded. "Nothing quite like a good persimmon."

"Nothing quite like it," my mom agreed. Then, for a moment, both looked wistfully into the distance as if they were imagining the best persimmon they'd ever had.

"It's so thoughtful of you to bring these." My mom snapped out of her mini daydream. I could tell she was impressed they came with something to share, just like the omiyage that Japanese people back home offered when visiting each other's houses. And that it wasn't junk food like cookies or neon-colored Fruit Roll-Ups (though I kind of liked those).

When Chloë and her father had rung the doorbell, my mom shapeshifted into Outside Mother, like the one she became when we were out and about. She stood up straighter, fixed her hair, and assumed her aloof-yet-alert air of someone in charge of something important when she opened the door.

However, within minutes of meeting Chloë's dad, I could tell my Outside Mother was relaxing into my regular mom. Mr. Yoshida's smile was open and wide, and he laughed easily.

Even though I already told her he didn't, my mom asked anyway. "Do you speak any Japanese?"

But instead of bristling defensively like I did when asked

this question, he just looked like a morose puppy.

"No, my Japanese is bad! It's so embarrassing. My grandparents learned from their parents, and they tried to encourage me, but I was so stubborn."

"You sound like Uriko," my mom replied.

Mr. Yoshida looked confused for a moment.

"Oh, that's Melony's real name," she explained. "She's Melony to people outside the home and Uriko—or sometimes Uri-chan—to us."

"She *is* like me!" Chloë's dad beamed. "My real name's Jouji, but everyone just calls me George. Melony"—Mr. Yoshida turned toward me and Chloë—"listen to your parents and learn as much Japanese as you can, okay? All I can say is 'Nice to meet you.' Hi-shew-my-mustache—wait, no, that's not it."

My parents traded looks. Then a sudden realization. "Hajimemashite?" my dad offered.

"That's it!" Mr. Yoshida exclaimed. "See? My Japanese is awful." And then he made a face so sad, it was funny.

My mom looked unsure, like she wanted very much to laugh at Mr. Yoshida's lousy Japanese, though she didn't want to be rude. But the twinkle in his eye invited her to. She giggled even though she tried to stop, and in trying to stop, she ended up snorting like a pig, which made both Chloë's dad and my mom erupt into full-blown guffaw ha-has. I couldn't believe it—he won my mom over within a few minutes, while it had taken Louisa's exceptionally patient and understanding parents over a year.

My dad, who happened to have the day off, hadn't laughed, though. He was still sizing up Mr. Yoshida and trying to decide whether he liked him or not. That's when Chloë's dad spotted the potato chip exhibit displayed in the glass case in the living room.

I tensed. Even though *I* humored my dad with figuring out what the weird-looking potato chips that he brought home from the factory resembled, I also knew it was kind of an odd hobby. And I didn't want Chloë's dad to think we were strange.

Mr. Yoshida gazed at the chips for a few seconds before he pointed to one in the top row.

"An owl?"

My dad raised an eyebrow. "That's right!"

"Mick Jagger of the Rolling Stones?" Mr. Yoshida pointed to the one next to it.

My dad nodded, surprised but still skeptical.

Mr. Yoshida pointed to the one that always seemed to make my dad sad. "Now, this one's interesting! It looks like someone—"

"Really?" my dad interrupted, his expression changing from skeptical to amazed. "I kept it because it reminded me of an old childhood friend. Who does it look like to you?"

"Oh, no one in particular." Chloë's dad looked embarrassed. "I was just going to say he looks like a friendly guy who's seen better days, I guess."

"Yes, that's exactly right," my dad answered glumly. "I thought that maybe you had known Jun somehow too."

Mr. Yoshida, realizing that maybe he had stepped into sensitive territory, cleared his throat and pointed to the newest addition. "This one has to be . . . the president?"

My dad snapped out of his gloom with a huge smile.

I let out a sigh of relief—it was pretty clear Chloë's dad had made a good impression on my parents. "Wanna see my room?" I asked Chloë.

She nodded and turned to her dad. "You're gonna leave soon, right?"

I flinched a little when my friend talked to her dad this way. I wondered how many points Chloë lost in my parents' mental scorebook.

But my parents and Mr. Yoshida all laughed instead, like Chloë had just told the funniest joke in the world. "I'll pick you up at five," he responded, but then frowned. "If that's all right with you. I could pick her up earlier, too."

My parents seemed surprised but also pleased that this new visitor didn't presume to leave his daughter at someone else's house for as long as possible. "Five is fine." My mother nodded.

Whatever points Chloë might have lost, Mr. Yoshida helped earn them back double in my parents' minds.

I scurried down the hall and motioned for Chloë to follow. She dashed behind me, and as soon as she was in my room, I closed the door like we were being chased. We giggled like we had just escaped a fate worse than death—hanging out with parents.

Once Chloë caught her breath, she looked around. "Why don't you have anything on your walls?" she asked.

"We're just renting this place, so my parents didn't want to put holes in them." I shrugged like it was no big deal. Truth is, I wanted more than anything to hang movie posters and artwork and photos and feathers and lots of other random things on my plain, dusty-blue walls, but I didn't want *her* to know that. Not yet, anyway.

"I like it—it's kind of like being in a cloudless sky," Chloë responded as she sat down on my bed. "Hey, are you going on the school band trip? I'm not sure I want to go yet."

Not sure? I almost tripped over myself. "Why *wouldn't* you want to go?" I asked.

"On the registration form, it says to list up to six people you want to room with at the hotel, but I barely know anyone. Can I list you?" She looked up at me expectantly. "If you're going, I'll go too."

"I, uh . . ." I still hadn't asked my parents for permission. Because, sometimes, not knowing the answer is better than being rejected outright. But when I took my time to reply, Chloë's expression changed from hope to disappointment. It was then I realized she thought I was going to turn down her roommate request.

"My parents are weird," I rushed to explain. "They don't even know about it yet."

Chloë's eyes grew wide. "Why not?"

"They treat me like a baby," I grumbled. "Me going on a three-day overnight trip might give them a heart attack. You wouldn't *believe* what they tell me about where I came from." And then, for the first time ever, I told a friend about how I was supposedly born from a melon.

When I was finished, I waited. In my mind, how she reacted would determine if this friendship stood a chance.

Chloë nodded seriously. "Maybe it's a metaphor."

We were learning all about metaphors and similes in Mr. Sutton's class.

"Oh yeah?" I had never considered this before. "A metaphor for what?"

"That . . . I do not know." Chloë looked thoughtful. "My parents used to tell me that they made me from straw and milk chocolate."

"What?" A giggle escaped me at the image that popped into my head.

"I know!" Chloë broke out into a huge grin. "Parents are so bizarre. But I bet they'll agree to let you go."

"I don't know," I groaned. "Even if I can't, you should. Don't you miss California?"

I'm not sure if Chloë heard me, though, because she didn't answer. Instead, she pulled her phone from her pocket and asked, "Hey, do you want to see some of my videos?"

I practically started drooling when I saw her phone. As far as I could tell, it looked like the newest, shiniest, most camera-est version of the best mobile phone that was out there. The rubbery case that protected it was covered in a sparkly flower design.

And then she handed it right over to me like she was sharing an extra piece of random fruit from her lunch. Like it wasn't the most precious prize she'd ever owned.

"Is this *your* phone?" My hands practically shook as I took it from her and watched a stop-motion video she had made.

This time it was her turn to shrug like it was nothing. "Kind of, I guess. My mom got a new one for her birthday, so I got her old one since my sister already has her own."

So many phones . . . It was hard for me not to feel jealous, but it was only for a second. Because then I laughed. Her videos were really funny!

Chloë burst into another huge grin and peered over my shoulder. "Wait, which one are you watching? We can make a new one if you want!"

Want? If *I want?* Of course I wanted to!

Chloë took the phone back from me. "We can make a stop-motion movie like that one. Or . . . do you want to learn a dance? There's one I wanted to learn and post, but I felt silly just doing it by myself."

There were a lot of kids at school who—without warning—burst into wiggles in the middle of the hall. At first I thought they were just being weird, but when a lot of them were flinging their arms and legs about in the same way, I figured it was some fad or trend I'd never find out about because my parents wouldn't let me.

"Which one?" I asked.

Chloë *tap, tap, tapped* and showed me the dance she wanted to learn. Looked easy enough. Stir like you're mixing something, clap, slide to the side, and then . . . everything got a little more complicated.

"Don't worry," Chloë said as she placed her phone where we both could see it. "We can work on it in pieces."

We stood in front of my thin full-length mirror that I had propped up on my floor and made our way through the dance. Stopping, starting, and playing back each move so many times we lost count. Sometimes we slid the wrong way and bumped into each other, but it didn't matter. We were having so much fun! That is, until my mom knocked on the door.

"Uri-chan, Chloë," she said. "Are you all right? You've been in there for over an hour. Don't you want some fresh air?"

Over an hour? It felt like it had only been a few minutes.

When my mom opened the door, Chloë hid her phone behind her back. It was hard for me to keep from smiling because she did it like it was a reflex. A twelve-year-old-girl reflex to a parent—any parent—entering her room. I would have done the exact same thing. That is, if I had a phone (which I didn't), even if I wasn't doing anything wrong (which I wouldn't be because . . . well, I'm not allowed to).

"Sure!" Chloë responded sweetly to my mom. She slipped

her phone into her back pocket, smooth as anything. "Wanna play hide-and-seek?"

Truth is, I hadn't played hide-and-seek since I was in elementary school, and the kids never played it at recess anymore. So, my first thought was that it was a "baby game," but you know what? I actually did want to play.

"Let's go in the backyard!" I suggested as I scooched past my mom, who still loomed in the doorway. Chloë followed me, but I noticed that—unlike me—she squeaked, "Excuse me!" as she passed by her.

Once we were outside, Chloë looked around our backyard, which was filled with overgrown trees and bushes and a gravel path that wound around them. It was kind of a mess, to be honest, and part of me worried she would be judgy about it.

"Whoo? Whoo? Who?" an owl hooted as if demanding to know the name of this new intruder.

We looked up into the trees, and, lo and behold, there was an owl that looked very much like the one I had named Bob years ago.

It ruffled its mottled brown-and-ivory feathers as it turned its cream-colored face toward us. I should have been happy to see Bob again, but something about the way he gripped us in his black-eyed, unblinking gaze unnerved me. It wasn't like he was just observing our antics, but more like he was *studying* us, and Chloë in particular.

Chloë didn't seem to notice, though. She just grinned.

"You have owls here?" she asked. "Lucky! I've never seen one so close before." She surveyed our yard again. "I can tell there are a *lot* of great places to hide. Do you want to be It?"

"Sure!" I agreed as I shook off the eeriness of the owl's stare. "To ten?"

"How about twenty?" Chloë said, dashing away before I could answer.

I covered my eyes and began counting. "One Mississippi, two Mississippi, three . . ."

In the darkness, I heard Chloë's footsteps running toward the right and crunching through the dead leaves we had yet to sweep up. Then there was a pause and silence.

Chloë's footsteps again, this time toward the left.

I bet she's hiding behind the Japanese maple, I thought as I continued to count. "Ten Mississippi, eleven Mississippi . . ."

"Who? Who?" Bob asked again. . . . At least, I thought it was Bob. He sounded hollow this time, though, almost like an echo of a real owl. I couldn't help but peek through my fingers toward the trees where I heard him.

He had moved onto a different branch, even closer this time. His eyes glittered and glowed in a way I'd never noticed in any owl before. When I gasped, he flapped his wings and took off into the darkening sky.

A giggle from the far end of the yard brought me back to the hide-and-seek game at hand. "Ready or not, here I come!" I called out. I hustled toward where I thought my friend was.

But when I peeked behind the trunk of the red maple, she

wasn't there, even though the crimson leaves quivered like someone had just brushed by them.

Bloodred. My mom's creepy description and how I felt when the owl locked us in his gaze made my breath catch in my throat. I forced myself to breathe out. Slowly. How silly I was being!

As I searched around the back corner of our property, there was a laugh behind me, then in front.

I whipped around, trying to spot where Chloë could be and wondering how she could be everywhere at once.

"Ha HA ha haha HA . . . HA hahahaha . . ." My friend's laughter bounced off the trees and echoed all around. A chill crept over me, and it wasn't just the type of cold that grew more intense when the sun went down—it was a prickling sensation that caused all the hairs on the back of my neck to rise.

"Chloë, stop it!" I yelled. I was frustrated I couldn't find my friend even in my own backyard. "Where are you?"

"What's going on here?" The old man from the house with the persimmon tree appeared, seemingly out of nowhere. I almost jumped out of my skin when I saw his scowling face behind the chain-link fence. The streetlight had just turned on, and its orange glow not only reflected off his balding head, it deepened the cracks and crevices of the wrinkles that lined his ancient face. My mom was right—he *was* scary.

Then, from behind the stack of firewood by our back door, Chloë jumped out. "Here I am!" she chirped. I ran toward her and away from my old neighbor so I didn't have to answer his question.

None of her giggles had come from that direction at all. I looked around, shaken. *How did she do that?* I wondered.

"That's where you were?" I asked. "The whole time?"

Chloë frowned. "Of course! Switching places in the middle of hide-and-seek is cheating. I'd never do that."

I took a deep breath. I'd only known Chloë a short time, but I knew my friend was telling the truth. So had I imagined all the strange laughter that hopped and skipped around the yard? I must have.

I slowly exhaled. "You wanna have some snacks now?" I asked.

"Sure!" Chloë responded. I got the sense she was agreeable to almost everything, but especially snacks.

Once inside, the tartness of the bright orange clementines that Mr. Yoshida brought chased away the creeping panic and confusion I felt just moments ago. Snacks made everything better.

"Are you girls having fun?" my mom asked as she walked by the kitchen on her way to the living room.

"Yep!" we both answered at the same time.

And I meant it. Hide-and-seek panic aside, this was the most fun I'd had in a long time.

"Hey, wanna take a selfie?" Chloë asked after my mom had left the room.

"Uh, sure," I replied.

Chloë held out her phone and we squished together. She tapped her phone several times and we checked the photos. We looked awful! But so much so that we laughed.

"Our selfie game—" Chloë began.

"Is craptastic!" I finished the sentence for her.

"Kora!" my mom scolded from the next room.

Chloë and I looked at each other and burst into another fit of giggles.

"She doesn't let you say 'crap'?" asked Chloë.

I shook my head. "She doesn't let me do a *lot* of things," I answered. "Don't *your* parents care if you say that word?"

Chloë shrugged. "I don't think they would. But I don't usually use it anyway, so I guess I wouldn't know."

My poor mom—if she thought "crap" was bad, her mind would explode if she knew what kind of language all the other middle schoolers used. All of them except maybe Chloë here.

We tried another selfie. And another. Finally, we had one photo that we both agreed was "not bad."

"There." Chloë tapped on the image to "favorite" it. "Now I have a photo of when we became true friends."

Chapter SEVEN

M y parents approved of Chloë Yoshida 100 percent, just like I knew they would.

"She's a very nice girl," my mom remarked. "Very polite."

"She's smart too," my dad added. "Mr. Yoshida said she could play three instruments!"

I could play three instruments, too, if I had more. An uninvited voice that took me by surprise popped up into my head. But it was silenced when my parents announced they'd be fine with letting me go over to my new friend's house next Friday.

And Chloë's place was everything I imagined it would be . . . and more!

When we arrived, their dog, Kiko, greeted us at the door, and sure enough, he looked like a fox—a dapper one with a fancy purple bandanna and a curly tail. He barked at me when Chloë opened the door.

"Here, come inside, quick! And close the door behind you or else he'll run away," Chloë instructed as she held on tight to his collar. "He's a total escape artist. Don't take it personally if he doesn't let you pet him right away. It takes him a while to warm up."

I couldn't think of anything worse than this cute curly-tailed dog not wanting to be my friend. So, after I stepped inside, I let him come to me, and even though I really wanted to give him a jowly rub, I stayed still as he sniffed me. And when he finally seemed ready, I gently scritched him under the collar, which he seemed to enjoy very much. I'd always wanted to have a dog, but of course my parents had a million excuses as to why we couldn't.

After I'd given him pets for a few minutes, Kiko looked straight into my eyes, smiled, and then pawed his nose. He looked at me again.

"Is there something on your nose?" I asked him as I rubbed his muzzle.

"No, but there is on yours!" laughed Chloë. "Look!" She pointed to the mirror hanging in their foyer. Sure enough, there was a smudge of dirt, which I hastily rubbed away. Kiko gave me a wide, toothy grin.

"He likes you!" Chloë seemed just as relieved as I was that Kiko had granted me his paw-stamp of approval. "He doesn't care for some people at all."

Chloë's room had blue walls like mine, but a brighter

shade, and they were decorated with posters of all sorts of different things. A werewolf in one, a space shuttle to the moon in another. A singer that lots of our classmates swooned over, and a bunch of rainbows, unicorns, and narwhals sprinkled throughout. If I had to figure out what kind of kid Chloë was based on how she decorated her room, I'm not sure I'd be able to. But I kind of liked the fact that she didn't fit in any sort of box.

"Wanna work on our dance some more?" Chloë asked as she propped her phone up on her neatly organized white desk.

"Sure!" I agreed. Even though we hadn't had a chance to practice for the entire week, we were much better than we were at my house.

"I think we're ready to record!" Chloë announced. We had a few false starts, but we finally were able to finish our dance without making many noticeable mistakes. "Should we post it?" Chloë played the recording as she handed her phone over to me. "Or do you think we should try one more time?"

Before I could answer, Mr. Yoshida knocked on the door. "Girls?" I put the phone behind my back just like Chloë did when she was at my house. "How are you doing? Are you hungry? Do you want something to eat?"

When Chloë's dad came in the room, he was holding a small string instrument.

"What's that?" I blurted out at the same time as Chloë said, "No, we're all good, Dad!"

Mr. Yoshida acted like he'd only heard me. "What, this? This is my ukulele!" He beamed.

"I've never seen one that looks like that," I answered before Chloë could shoo him away. It was covered in a dark carved design and shaped more like an egg.

"It's a pineapple body," Chloë's dad said proudly. My friend had her arms crossed and her fingers tapped impatiently. Maybe sensing he would be banished soon, Mr. Yoshida talked quickly. "I have another one downstairs. Would you like to try it?"

"Sure!" I agreed as I shot Chloë an apologetic glance. I mouthed, "Brownie points" to her so she knew that I was just doing this to get her parents to like me. Her annoyed look changed into an approving one and she gave me a quick nod. "Good thinking," she whispered.

Truth is, I *did* kinda want to learn. It might be boring for her since she already knew how to play three instruments, including the French horn she played for the school band. But I only knew how to play the piccolo, and—if I'm being perfectly honest—not well.

Down in their living room, there was an upright piano and the second ukulele—this one painted with a cascading blue wave on it—hanging on the wall. Mr. Yoshida handed me the pineapple ukulele as he grabbed the other one for himself. Chloë *fwumped* down on the piano bench. I tried to ignore that she was clearly feeling impatient toward her dad for hijacking our playdate, even though that's not what it was since we don't call it that in middle school anymore.

"But . . ." I wasn't even sure how to hold the ukulele, I was so worried I would break it. "I don't know how to play."

"Yet!" Mr. Yoshida smiled.

"Anyone can learn how to play ukulele!" Chloë's annoyance seemed to have passed. She played a scale up and down on the piano.

"It's true! If you know four chords, you can play almost anything." When Chloë's dad plucked his ukulele, he made it seem like the easiest thing in the world to make the most cheerful, bright tune burst forth. It immediately made me think of warm winds and palm trees. Its rhythm reminded me of waves splashing onto golden sands.

When Mr. Yoshida began to sing, I couldn't understand a single word he said. But it sounded like happiness.

"Ugh, Dad, enough with the Hawaiian music!" Chloë complained. "How about something all of us can sing?"

Mr. Yoshida winked, and without missing a beat, he transitioned into "What a Wonderful World."

The music even brought Chloë's older sister out from her lair. Her name was Emily, and according to Chloë, she spent most of the time in her room FaceTiming her friends, but with the camera pointing at the ceiling. Which didn't make any sense at first, but when we walked by her room when I first arrived, I couldn't help but notice how disastrously messy it was. Clothes piled on the floor, dresser drawers half open. Crumpled-up candy bar wrappers near her trash bin, and a strand of skull-shaped lights framing her window. If my room looked like that, I guess I wouldn't want any of my friends to see it, either! Chloë shook her head and muttered, "Teenagers" when she noticed me staring. Chloë also said Emily was bossy and moody, but to me she just seemed older and so cool. She had braces, and the blue rubber bands on them matched a blue streak in her short, dark hair. Now that she was in the living room with us, she acted like it was because she was just passing through and not that she actually wanted to be there. She casually took a guitar from its stand and sat down off to the side.

In no time at all, Chloë and her dad taught me a few basic chords and we sang a bunch of songs together, including ones about brown-eyed girls (like us) and another that asked if we'd ever seen the rain. Which of course we had, since we lived in Oregon!

I was one way with my parents and another way at school. With Chloë at the Yoshida home, I was yet another way. I don't know if it was quite myself, but it felt pretty close. In fact, in this house that felt larger and brighter than mine, with a dad who still had energy at the end of the week, and two other kids close to my age, I felt like an *even better* version of myself.

Then Chloë's mom came home. Not only was she pretty and dressed nicely, but more importantly, she carried in three boxes of pizza.

My parents think Americans eat too much pizza. We eat

it sometimes, but whenever we do, it's accompanied by comments such as "Too cheesy! So greasy!" And then my mom piles vegetables on it. Green pepper, onions, mushrooms— she even tried to sneak finely chopped broccoli onto it once.

If there's one surefire way to ruin a good pizza, it's broccoli.

Chloë's sister had taken the pizza boxes and opened them. One was just cheese, the other was pepperoni. The last one Hawaiian. Nothing green in sight (*yes!*).

"You must be Melony!" Mrs. Yoshida unwound her pink silk scarf in a way that seemed so glamorous. My own mom hardly ever accessorized. "We've heard so many wonderful things about you!"

So many? I blushed. I couldn't think of *any* remarkable things about myself that Chloë could have said.

"Mom, can Melony stay for dinner, please?" Chloë asked.

"Of course!" Mrs. Yoshida answered back right away. "I brought home enough pizza to feed an army."

"And . . ." Chloë motioned for her mom to come closer. Mrs. Yoshida leaned over, and she whispered into her mom's ear.

"Spend the night?" Mrs. Yoshida stood up. "It's a Friday, so I don't see why not. That is, if Melony would like to."

Chloë turned to me, the excitement shining in her eyes. "You wanna?" she asked. "We can stay up late watching horror films. That is, if you *like* scary movies."

Truth is, I'd never seen one. My parents said they'd give me nightmares.

"And I'll also make you whatever you want for breakfast." Mr. Yoshida hopped up to give Chloë's mom a hug. "What will it be? Waffles? Bacon? Pancakes in the shape of your initials?" he asked.

"We're not five, Dad," Chloë laughed. "We'll just pour ourselves some cereal."

Mr. Yoshida looked sad for a moment, then determined. "I can make *anything* for breakfast. I'm serious. Even . . . mashed potatoes with gravy."

Mashed potatoes with gravy? I'd never heard of anyone having *that* for breakfast. Still . . .

"Sure," I found myself answering. Out of the corner of my eye, I saw Chloë mouthing, "Brownie points" back at me and giving me another approving nod.

"It's settled, then!" Mrs. Yoshida fished her phone out from her purse. "Let's see if we can catch your mom before she comes to pick you up. Then maybe she can bring your sleepover stuff instead!"

Chloë and I traded grins. The truth is I had never slept over at a friend's house before. Louisa had asked if I could when we were seven, but my parents said that I was too young then. At the time, I asked, "When is not too young?" And my parents had said, "Twelve." Then Louisa moved away, so I didn't think to ask again. But now that I was twelve and I had a new friend, they would *have* to say yes.

Mrs. Yoshida searched her phone for our contact information, which my parents had made sure she had. I listened as Chloë's mom spoke to mine. "Oh, I see. . . . No, I understand. . . . Another time, then! Maybe during winter break . . . Would it be all right if she stayed for dinner, though? We'd love to have her. . . . Okay, wonderful! See you soon."

I did *not* like how that conversation sounded.

Chloë's mom set her phone down on the counter. "So, girls, it looks like tonight's not the best night. I guess your mother has a quilting show tomorrow?"

I nodded, but barely. It was taking all my self-control not to erupt like a volcano.

They promised. They promised that when I was older, I could spend the night at a friend's house.

"How nice of you to help your mom with that!" Chloë's mom continued. "It's great that you have a hobby you can share. Maybe someday Chloë will golf with me—what do you think, Chlo?" Mrs. Yoshida booped her daughter on her nose.

"Stop, Mom. Geez." Chloë pouted as she pushed her mom's hand away. "I'm not Kiko. Go boop his nose."

But instead of getting mad, her mom laughed. "Let's eat dinner so you can hang out some more before Melony has to go. Okay? Okay!"

Chapter EIGHT

On the ride back from Chloë's house, I barely said a word to my dad. I was afraid if I did, all my frustration would burst forth like a flood and drown us both.

Baby. Why did they treat me like one? I was *twelve*, people! This nonsense about the quilting convention tomorrow. That was clearly an excuse to destroy my fun, I just knew it.

When we arrived home, my face got warmer and warmer as my parents sat me down in the living room and explained that "staying up so late would only make you feel bad the following day" and "sleepovers weren't something that kids did in Japan."

"Be we're *not* in Japan! We're in Oregon, and kids in Oregon have sleepovers!"

Then they explained that they "like the Yoshidas, but we shouldn't impose."

"It wouldn't be imposing because they invited me!" I

fumed. "They wouldn't have invited me if they didn't want to have me over."

Even though my teeth were clenched when I answered, my response might have come out louder than I meant it to.

"Melony, don't raise your voice at your mother!" my dad yelled at me. "What's gotten into you?"

What's gotten into ME? I thought. *More like, what's gotten into YOU!*

"You promised, you promised, you promised!" Okay, so this time I definitely was yelling. "You said that when I was older, I could finally spend the night at a friend's house!"

"We did?" My parents acted all innocent like this was news to them. "When?"

"When Louisa asked five years ago. You said seven was too young, but I am *twelve* now! You said *if* I was good, and I have been very, extremely, super good!"

"You remember that?" Mom asked.

"I remember *everything*!" I raged.

"What's so wrong with staying here?" my dad asked weakly. "Would you really rather be over at the Yoshidas' than here?"

"I'd rather be *anywhere* but here!" The words came out faster than I could stop them. I dashed down the hall into my room, away from their shocked looks and suffocating ways.

I tossed and turned that night. When I finally did fall asleep, I dreamed of a mishmash of odd things, like the match from my birthday burning down to my fingers and singeing them; of our scary old neighbor creeping by our house; of climbing his persimmon tree; of someone—*something*—who looked like Chloë but was not Chloë hiding behind our Japanese red maple tree.

"Uri-chan?" my mom called from across the hall the following morning, just as the dark night was giving way to a wet and dreary dawn. "It's time to wake up if we want to get to the quilting show on time."

Mom might have wanted to act like nothing had happened, but I could not. I *would not*. So, I hatched a plan.

Cough, cough. I cleared my throat.

"Melony? Would you like to get ready for the show?" My dad knocked and then opened my door halfway. "Your mother is going to display her quilt that she's worked so hard on. And that you helped with too! Maybe it will even win an award!"

No way I'm going to some stupid ole boring quilting show, I thought. So I answered, "Sure," but followed up with an *ah-choo!* I grabbed some Kleenex from my nightstand and blew my nose as loudly as I could.

"Are you okay?" My dad sat on my bed and put his cool hand on my forehead. "You do feel a little warm."

My mom came into my room next. She batted my dad's arm away and checked my "fever" with her own palm. "Seems normal to me."

"I'm fine." I cleared my throat once more as I sat up. I

knew if I milked the "I'm sick" deception too hard, my parents might catch on. But then I sneezed again, for real this time.

Perfect timing.

"Should we let her stay home?" Dad asked. "We can't take a sick child to a quilting show. Everyone there is really old."

"Not everyone." Mom harrumphed.

"I'm sure it's just allergies." I gambled on the fact that my mom would disagree with me like she so often did these days.

"Even so, people will *think* you're sick, and . . ." Her voice trailed off.

You worry about what people think all the time, I finished my mom's thought for her. I lay back down again, with my back to my parents. Sure enough, she checked her watch and sighed. "Well, if you can't come with us, I'm expecting a package. So, try to get out of bed and bring it in if it arrives, all right?"

Wow, not even a "please" or a "hope you feel better," I thought. Funny how they're always on *my* case to remember my manners.

In protest, I acted like I'd fallen back asleep to avoid answering.

"Fine, sleep," my mom mumbled. Even without looking at her, I could tell she was a little disappointed. I started to feel a bit guilty about my mean thoughts, but then she added, "It's a good thing we didn't let you stay over at Chloë's. What if you had gotten her sick too?"

After that, I wished I *had* actually voiced my thoughts

instead of keeping them in like I always do.

"We should go," she said to my dad. "Or we'll be late." She got up and left my room in a hurry.

My dad waited behind, though. "Will you be okay by yourself?" he asked. "I could stay with you."

"I'm not *dying*," I muttered, my back still toward him.

He didn't answer, but I could tell he was still worried by the way he rested his hand on my head. "Feel better, all right?"

I pulled my covers higher.

My dad patted me again and stood up. "Make sure to call or text us, okay? We'll be back before dinner." I didn't respond because even though I knew his pats were meant to be reassuring, it felt as if he were treating me like a puppy instead.

"And don't forget to practice your piccolo!" my mom hollered right before they left.

"If you're feeling up to it," Dad added.

When I heard my parents' car start, I threw off my covers. I peeked out the window and watched the sheets of rain batter their car until it disappeared around the corner.

Funny thing about my parents is that they wouldn't let me spend the night at Chloë's, because sleepovers weren't something that happened in Japan. But they would let me stay at home by myself because babysitters aren't commonly hired in Japan, either. Combining that with the possibility that I could be sick, and their internet searches that confirmed children could stay by themselves for short periods of time starting at age ten, Mom's internal risk calculation—*bee bee beep, bee bee beep*—determined that I could at least have this day to myself.

And would I take advantage of my freedom? One hundred percent.

Instead of washing my face and changing into my clothes like I did every morning, I stayed in my pajamas and deliberately put on mismatched socks. In searching for a perfectly clashing pair, I threw a bunch of my other socks on the bedroom floor. As I was about to pick them up, I remembered Chloë's older sister's room and realized it wasn't messy for no reason. It was *defiantly* messy. I left everything on the floor and my dresser drawer half-open. *That'll show them!*

If this were any other morning, I would have put my hair up in a ponytail or woven it into a braid because my mom was always getting after me to "look neat." But since this was not like any other morning, I left it crazy and tangled, like a bowl of spaghetti dropped on the floor.

I almost tripped over my piccolo case as I was about to exit my bedroom. Remembering my mom's instructions not to forget to practice, I picked it up and set it on my bed. I still hadn't asked my parents if I could go on the overnight band trip, and I never would because I knew what they'd say. So, I didn't forget to practice. I *decided* not to.

For breakfast, I pulled out a box of the healthy, non-sugary, very wood chip–like breakfast cereal I usually ate on the weekends. I tried not to think about the mashed potatoes and gravy I'd be having over at the Yoshidas if my parents had let me stay. Even though that actually sounded kind of gross to me at the moment, it still didn't make me want to eat this box of good-for-you sawdust instead. I put the cereal back on the pantry shelf and decided a hot dog with neon-green relish and unnaturally yellow mustard sounded like the *perfect* breakfast to have today.

I turned on the TV and lounged on the sofa while I ate. I bit into my microwaved hot dog and immediately opened my mouth again. "Haaaah, haaah," I breathed as I tried to cool it down. All the stuff I had added to it dripped out of the bun and onto my pajama top. Did I care? Nope! I gulped down my first bite.

As I searched for the stupidest, most ridiculous show to watch—the kind my parents told me would "melt your brain"—I heard a *tap, tap, tapping* on the window.

I tried to ignore it, but the sound grew louder, from a tapping to almost a *knock, knock, knocking*. I stood up and peeked out the window.

"Is someone there?"

The knocking faded back into a tapping. No one answered.

The rain had stopped, at least for now, and the water *drip-dropped* from the gutters like tears. Maybe that's what I had heard.

Plink.

I sat back down and grabbed the remote. My hand still

had relish on it, so I reached for a tissue to clean up the mess. But then I stopped. I went to a restaurant with my mom and dad recently, and a woman and her very messy child were eating at the table next to us. By the time they left, the child had smeared mac 'n' cheese into his curls like hair gel, splatted his bright orange Jell-O onto the table, and hurled his jam-covered bread rolls onto the floor. But instead of cleaning up after themselves like *I'd* always been taught to, the woman murmured, "Cost of doing business!" to herself, picked up her kid, and left the waiters to clean up their mess.

My parents were *appalled*. But remembering this incident, I decided I wasn't going to clean up after myself, either. *This mess could have been at the Yoshidas*, I thought. *But you didn't want me to stay there, so* you *can deal with my mess.* Just like the woman at the restaurant, I murmured, "Cost of doing business!" and left the remote control sticky with relish.

And I relished how that felt.

Knock, knock, knock.

This time, there was no doubt there was someone at the door. I jumped up.

"Who's there?" I yelled.

"Who? Who? Who?"

I ran to the door and peeked out. I half expected to see Bob the Barred Owl, but there wasn't anything there.

Knock, knock, knock.

This time, it sounded like someone was at the back door. I ran to check.

"Who is it?" I called out.

No answer. Until . . .

"Who? Who isss . . . Who iss it?" The question was repeated back to me . . . *in my own voice.*

I took a step back. Was it . . . an *echo*? But it's not like that had ever happened before at my house. My whole body tensed.

"Whooooo's ready . . . for more slime?" an announcer called out from the TV. Then cheers from the audience.

I relaxed. *That's* what it was. Maybe the TV was messing with my brain, just like my parents said it would.

As I headed back to the living room to turn it off (and to clean up the smudge of relish on the remote control), a *kat-hunk* directed my attention back to the front porch.

Mom's package she'd told me to look out for.

I peeked out the door and there it was—a large, square brown box—like any other package on any other day.

Only it didn't have a return address and, in handwritten letters that looked like chicken-scratch, it was addressed to . . .

URIKO

That was really weird. No one called me Uriko except my parents, but they weren't ones for random surprises like this.

On its side was a white sticker with the word "FRAGILE" on it. Which only made me more suspicious and more curious at the same time.

But Mom *did* tell me to bring the package in . . . so, I

opened the door and looked around.

There was no delivery truck in sight, which was double weird because it had *just* been dropped off.

I grabbed the box and carried it inside. It was heavy, almost like it was filled with books, or sand, or *something* hefty and weighty like that. But it said "FRAGILE," and those weren't fragile things.

Should I open it? Part of me wondered if I should wait until my parents came back. My mom had told me to look out for the package, but she didn't say I could open it.

She didn't say I *couldn't* open it, either.

Before I could change my mind, I grabbed a pair of scissors and sliced at the tape holding the box closed.

Whoosh. A gust of wind seemed to rise up from the slit in the box and blow past my face. *That's strange. . . .*

I opened the flaps to reveal . . .

Nothing. Absolutely nothing at all.

I took the box and shook it upside down. Still nothing. I set it back on the table.

"Uuu-riii . . . ," a raspy voice called out softly from behind me. "U . . . ri . . . ko . . ."

I tensed up and whipped around, but when I did, a fuzzy gray creature—kind of like a person in a wolf suit, but not quite; sort of like a Muppet, but not as cheerful or brightly colored—

Was

Standing

In
My
Kitchen.

I screamed at the top of my lungs and staggered back toward the counter.

"I'm sorry, did I startle you?" it asked. "I didn't mean to."

Was I dreaming? Could this really be happening? I closed my eyes and tried to shake myself awake. When I opened them, it was still there.

I raised my fists. "Who are you? Get out of my house!" I'd never gotten in a fight before, but the ones I'd seen on TV often started out like this. "Who are you?" I yelled again. "*What* are you?"

The gray creature lowered its round, glowing eyes. It recited sadly: "I am neither here nor there. Neither person nor beast. Anyone or anything. I am neither house nor truck, fork nor spoon . . ." It went on for a minute or two, reciting what it was not. "I am neither pencil nor pen, high nor low, north nor south, east nor west."

After the initial surprise and rush of seeing this creature appear *like magic* in my home, I began to feel very tired. "One thing's for certain," I interrupted as I lowered my arms. "You *are* very annoying."

"Oh." The thing's narrow shoulders slumped, and the tips of its fuzzy pointed ears drooped slightly. "Am I? I'm very sorry, Uriko." And then it made a face so sad that it reminded me of Mr. Yoshida's when he admitted he couldn't speak Japanese. Although I was extremely alarmed when it first appeared, it actually seemed quite harmless now. It was only a couple inches taller than me and had a poochy belly, like a baby.

I certainly hadn't invited this creature into my house, but I felt sorry that I'd been rude and unwelcoming. I softened my tone. "Could you please just tell me what you are and not what you aren't? I think you'd get to the point quicker that way. And don't call me Uriko— my name's Melony. Come to think of it, how do you even know my old name anyway?"

The creature met my eyes, its pointy ears perking up. "All right, then, Melony—I'm Jack Amano!"

Jack Amano? It hadn't answered my question about how it knew I was Uriko, but I racked my brain for what that name—*Jack Amano*—should mean to me. I couldn't come up with anything.

"You're acting like I should know you." I crossed my arms. "I don't."

It rubbed its three-fingered paws together nervously. "I mean, you might have heard of my other name?"

"Oh yeah? What's that?"

"Some people call me Amanojaku. Or Amanjaku."

Amanjaku. Where had I heard this name before? *Amanjaku.* Suddenly, I remembered.

I started shaking. From the shock and realization that my parents had been telling me the truth, and that this creature was so close that I could almost touch it.

"You're that evil demon who hurt that boy from my dad's village!" I snarled.

"What? No! That's not who I am," the Amanjaku replied earnestly. "I did no such thing. Did they really say that?"

I wished, for a moment, that I hadn't been so quick to dismiss them. That I hadn't tuned my parents out as soon as they started telling me stories of their past, and that I had listened a little more closely. "I . . . I guess not exactly. They said that you made a boy in the village do bad things—"

"While it's true that the boy and I were friends," the guest interrupted, "that boy did all those naughty things on his own. He was just a bad egg." It cocked a bushy eyebrow as if suspicious of me and took a step back. "Are *you* a bad egg?"

I frowned. "Well, no, but—"

"Then you have nothing to worry about. Your parents might have heard rumors about me, but they don't really *know* me." And then it looked sad again.

My fists were lowered, but I clenched them again. "Oh yeah? If you're not so bad, then why'd you lie and tell me your name was Jack Amano?"

The Amanjaku looked confused. "I didn't lie! I just wanted to be like you. I thought 'Jack Amano' sounded . . . I dunno. Friendlier. It's easier to pronounce than 'Amanjaku,' don't you think? You used to be Uriko, but now you're Melony, right? How's that any different?"

I thought it was awfully audacious for this demon thing to not only barge into my house, but to be all nosy about my name. "I can pronounce 'Amanjaku' just fine," I retorted. I was a little sensitive about my Japanese since my parents corrected my mistakes from time to time. "What do you want?" I asked in a way that I hoped showed the Amanjaku just how unwelcome it was.

"I . . . I just want to play. Surely you can understand where I'm coming from?" And then before my very eyes, the Amanjaku began to change.

First, its fuzzy ears shrank and became more rounded.

Then long black hair grew on its head. The rest of its fur appeared to melt and then smooth out into what looked like . . . clothes?

What in the world??

In only a few seconds, the Amanjaku morphed into something—I mean *someone*—who very much resembled my good friend Chloë.

"Hey!" I put my guard down completely and walked around the Amanjaku. "How'd you do that? That's not really you, is it, Chloë?

"Do I look like her?" the Amanjaku replied in a voice that was a *whole lot* like Chloë's, only it was slightly hollow. "I tried my best. It was dark when I saw her, though. You know, when you were playing that game. What was it called? 'Find Me, Find Me'?"

"Hide-and-seek," I corrected. "You were there?" I tried to remember the details from that night. I gasped. "Bob?"

"Bob? Who's that?" The Amanjaku giggled. "I don't know

who that is, but I can be whoever you want me to be. At least for a little while. And you wanted to play, right?"

"Yeah, but . . ." I scratched my head. "Everyone knows we don't 'play' anymore in middle school."

"We can hang out, then. Aren't you bored here by yourself?" New Chloë held a darker version of Real Chloë's sparkly, flowery phone. "Don't you think your parents would rather you did anything other than . . ." She glanced toward the TV, where someone was leaping into a vat of cereal after having rolled themselves in Marshmallow Fluff. "That?"

It had a point. I took the phone from the Amanjaku and turned on the screen. Maybe it was just me, but it seemed to glow brighter and clearer than the one Real Chloë had. It was almost like the images were 3D and they were pulling me in.

Sure, it was very strange how this creature appeared in my house in a box. But I wouldn't have even been here if my parents had let me stay over at Chloë's. If they had let me have a real phone, I might be catching up with Louisa and looking at all the wonderful places she's traveled to. What else did they expect me to do? Sit here by myself and practice my piccolo for a trip they'd never let me go on?

"All right, then," I agreed. "But only until my parents come home."

First, New Chloë and I watched silly videos and laughed and laughed for about an hour. They were mostly of dogs being cute and clumsy or cats acting all hoity-toity before falling off a kitchen table and then bouncing right back up like they had meant to do that. Harmless stuff like that. There was one with a ridiculous boy on a skateboard who held on to the side of a car as his friend drove it down the street. Then the boy let go and tried to use the momentum to do an "epic" trick (his word, not mine) on his skateboard but wiped out *hard* on the pavement. He lay there in a crumpled heap and didn't move.

New Chloë chortled and guffawed until she was almost crying.

I laughed, too, once the boy got up and I saw that he was okay. Like the cats we were watching earlier, he stood and acted like wiping out was all part of his plan.

New Chloë seemed disappointed by this, or maybe bored, because she let out a huge yawn. "What do you want to do now?" she asked.

It had stopped raining and now a patch of sun shone through the remaining clouds. That didn't happen very often in late-autumn mornings in Oregon.

"The park?" New Chloë suggested after I couldn't come up with anything.

"Yeah!" I jumped up, but then stopped.

"What? Don't you want to go?" my new friend asked innocently.

"It's just that my parents don't usually let me go by myself," I explained. "Plus, they'd be super mad I let a stranger in the house in the first place."

"You wouldn't be by yourself, though. I'd be with you, and I'm not a stranger. They told you themselves that they already know me." New Chloë seemed genuinely puzzled. "Why won't they let you go? It's just around the corner. Don't they trust you?"

My face grew warm as I thought of my parents and how they hardly let me do anything. "They treat me like a baby." I glowered.

"You're not a baby!" New Chloë giggled like she couldn't imagine anyone being so silly as to think such a thing.

"You're right. I'm definitely old enough to go to the park, I don't care what they think—" Then I looked down at my pj's. "But I can't go like this."

My visitor looked confused. "Why not?"

"Because people don't go to the park in their pajamas," I tried to explain. "What if someone saw me and—" I stopped, realizing I'd just mentioned I didn't care what my parents thought.

New Chloë still didn't seem to understand.

"Just wait here while I change," I instructed.

She shrugged, like she was already getting tired of our time together. "Suit yourself."

I rushed into my room and dug my favorite shirt out from the bottom of my drawer. It was *my* favorite shirt, but not my parents'. It was faded and ripped, which *I* thought made it cool, but my parents said it made us look like they couldn't afford to dress me properly. So, it was *the* best outfit for today.

At the park, New Chloë let me use her phone to take pictures. I took close-ups of a slug sliming its way across the sidewalk, of an autumn leaf that was green in the middle but changing to red, then yellow at the tips. She wouldn't let me take any of her, though.

"I'm shy," New Chloë explained. "I never like how I look in photos, either."

I nodded. Lots of kids at the school, girls especially, took selfie after selfie and posted them online only after cropping the image and applying the perfect filter. I thought she looked fine, but I cringed at almost every photo I saw of myself, so I knew where New Chloë was coming from. The selfie that Real Chloë and I had taken when we became friends was practically the only one I'd liked recently.

When a drop of water hit my face, I wasn't sad. New Chloë and I had had an awesome time at the park, but now I was tired, and the rain reminded me that I was hungry too. The hot dog with relish and mustard was the only thing I'd had all day, and it was already well past noon.

"Come on—it's starting to rain!" I dashed back home with New Chloë close behind.

Once back inside, I asked, "Want a snack?"

"Sure!" my guest agreed, just like Real Chloë would have. "Whatever is easiest."

I wondered what would be good to serve on a rainy autumn day like today. Normally, my mom always handled snacks. Not because I couldn't but so she could make sure that they were always healthy. For some reason, I felt weirdly anxious having to figure this out on my own. But then I had the *best* idea. I found two mugs and filled them with milk. I heated them up in the microwave for a minute and a half and stirred in a heaping tablespoon of hot chocolate mix to each. I set one cup in front of my guest and warmed my hands with the other.

When my tummy rumbled, I remembered I should probably find something for us to *eat*, too. I rummaged through the cabinet and found some chocolate chip cookies. My parents usually only let me have a hot chocolate *or* chocolate chip cookies, never both at once. But today I had a visitor over, from *Japan*, even, so it made sense in my mind to serve her something a little extra.

I set out two cookies for each of us and finally sat down to eat my snack with New Chloë. But by the time I'd taken a bite of one cookie and three sips of hot chocolate, she had already completely finished!

"That was delicious." New Chloë patted her stomach. But then she looked around hungrily, like a lion searching for unsuspecting antelopes nearby.

I wasn't sure what to do. Hot chocolate with chocolate chip cookies did seem like a lot of sugar at once, but my guest seemed to want more.

"Are you still hungry? Would you like another one . . . or two?" I decided to at least offer.

"Oh no. I don't want to take more than my share," New Chloë answered. But her stomach growled loudly like a train roaring through a dark tunnel.

"We still have plenty," I insisted. I checked out the label on the bag of cookies. "Says here that one serving is actually five cookies!"

"Five cookies?" my new friend squealed. "Well then, I guess I wouldn't mind having a few more."

I gave New Chloë three more cookies, and in less than a second, they were gone. I hurried to finish my snack as well.

As I was about to get up and clear our dishes, New Chloë asked, "Aren't you going to have a full serving of cookies? I would feel bad if I ate so many more cookies than you."

I didn't want my friend to feel awkward about having a healthy appetite, so I helped myself to three more too. But it felt weird to have her just sit there while I rushed to wolf down my cookies.

"Uh . . ." I racked my brain for what else I could offer. "You wouldn't happen to want any potato chips, would you?" With my dad's job, that was something we always had on hand but I hardly ate because we were all tired of them. I know that sounds weird—I mean, who gets tired of potato chips? But, believe me, if you had them available twenty-four seven for as long as you could remember, you'd be bored of them too.

Luckily, it was love at first crunch for my new friend. They were a special kettle corn flavor, too—both salty *and* sweet. I still had to gobble up my cookies way faster than I normally would since New Chloë consumed her chips in no seconds flat. She liked them so much, she tilted her head back and poured the crumbs straight into her wide-open mouth.

And then . . . SUGAR RUSH! Even though my parents didn't like it when I ran inside the house, that's what we did. After all, they weren't here, and we had *so much energy*. We bounced on the sofa, had a pillow fight with its cushions, and buzzed down the hall.

Then my phone—my *real* cell phone—rang, and we stopped. I knew it was my parents because it was that type of super-boring cell phone that parents first get for their five-year-old kids, with a bunch of parental controls on it and just a few contacts saved. No fun at all! The only people who had my number were my parents, Louisa, and Chloë. Most parents upgrade their kids' phones after a year or two, but did mine? No way! And my old friend's calls and texts petered out a couple months after she left. I stopped trying, too, because Louisa was always in the middle of something or a place where the cell service was bad, so my call would go straight to voice mail. Or my text would go unanswered for hours, sometimes even days. And my new friend wouldn't be calling me because she was right here. . . . It seemed like she was, anyway.

"Hello?" I answered my phone.

The good news was that my parents were bringing home apple pie. The bad news was that they were only fifteen minutes away. Normally, that information would have filled my heart with songs of joy. If there was one thing I liked even more than cookies, it was apple pie. But at the moment, this information made me feel a little sick. Probably because I couldn't imagine eating even *more* treats.

Not only that, but the state that the house was in filled me with dread. Sofa cushions on the ground. Cookie crumbs everywhere and hot chocolate drips on countertops. The day's excitement diminished like morning dew in the hot sun, and for the first time since the Amanjaku had arrived, I questioned what kind of friend would take part in trashing my home like this. What had I done? Even though I'd had a ton of fun earlier, right about now I was really wishing I hadn't let the Amanjaku in. When my parents saw this disaster, they would ground me for life without parole.

"Oh no." I panicked. "Oh no, oh no, oh no. What are we going to do?"

"Clean, silly!" New Chloë remarked. I stood back as my guest zipped to and fro like a whirlwind. She swept, wiped, dusted, and straightened. In less than five minutes, the room was as it used to be, maybe even better.

I felt a little bad for having doubted her earlier.

My new friend patted its fuzzy brow and panted like a dog on a hot day.

"Are you all right?" I asked it. The effort it took to clean seemed to override the Amanjaku's Chloë disguise.

"Making myself look like someone I'm not takes some

effort, especially at first. I know you understand." The Amanjaku sat down at the kitchen table as it caught its breath. "I had a great time! Did you?"

All my earlier regrets had disappeared along with the mess. "I did!" I answered even as I wondered what the Amanjaku meant when it said I would "understand" about disguising myself as someone I wasn't.

But before I could say anything, it asked, "Then we'll play again, right?"

"Um, not 'play.' Middle schoolers 'hang out,' remember?" I responded.

Before the Amanjaku could say anything else, my parents' car pulled into our driveway.

"Quick, you have to go!" I urged . . . to no one at all. My guest was nowhere to be seen—the only evidence that it was even there was the fancy phone it had let me use earlier.

I grabbed it off the kitchen table and hid it behind my back just as my parents walked in.

"Oh, Melony! It looks like you are feeling better?" My dad greeted me cheerfully as he set the apple pie down on the kitchen table.

"Yes, much!" I answered. "How was the show?" I slipped the new phone into my back pocket.

My mom entered the house then, her purse in one hand, a blue ribbon in the other. "Not bad," she smiled as she set the ribbon next to the pie. It was like the fight we had last night never happened.

My mom looked around. "No package, huh?"

I shook my head.

"Probably Monday, then. How about you?" my mom asked. "What did you do today?"

"Oh, nothing much," I answered before I could stop myself. I felt a twinge of remorse for lying to them, first about the package (besides, I'm *sure* she wasn't talking about the box the Amanjaku came in!) and then about not doing anything today.

I prepared some tea for my parents to make myself feel better. When I set the cups in front of them, I could tell they felt better too. With this peace offering, our fight from yesterday was behind us.

But how could I explain to them that the Amanjaku they warned me about had been in our house . . . and that it wasn't the least bit bad?

My mom's left eyebrow rose when she noticed the old, ripped shirt I was wearing. "Hmm." She sniffed. "That's fine for the weekend, I guess."

I decided it was better not to mention the Amanjaku at all.

didn't see the Amanjaku again, at least for the next few days. Part of me was relieved, but another part of me couldn't help but long for the fun we had together. Later, when I was by myself in my bedroom, I reached into my back pocket for the phone that the Amanjaku had left, but that was gone too. I began to wonder if I had actually woken up at all that morning or if its visit was just a dream. By the following week, I'd fully returned to my routine: Wake up. Eat breakfast. Boring classes. Hang out with Chloë during lunch and recess. Tolerate ear-splitting music during band. Find Mr. Sutton's class mildly interesting. Get picked up. Home. Repeat, etc., etc.

But on Tuesday, life became decidedly more exciting. Because the Amanjaku showed up—this time in band class.

Miasma and Scat were up to their usual nonsense. We were supposed to spend the first five minutes of class getting ready for our end-of-quarter duet test, but instead, they had traded instruments (again) and were practicing that way. The tuba/piccolo combination was an odd pairing to begin with, but their switcheroo made them particularly awful today. The instructor, Ms. Delgado, wasn't saying anything because she was busy preparing her soundproof office and testing area over to the side of the main band room so she could listen to each pair separately.

When Chloë walked into class a minute after the bell rang, I was about to give her a hard time for being tardy. But then I noticed she was sniffling and her eyes were red.

"Chloë?" I whispered. "What . . . what's wrong? Did something happen?" I'd thought since we had become friends so quickly, she'd be spared any sort of bullying because she was new.

No such luck. *No one* leaves the new kid alone.

But before today, nothing seemed to bother her. Like that time when we walked around the track and the boys hollered Pokémon stuff at us. She thought it was a little odd, but she wasn't offended by them. She just shrugged it off. In my research about owls in Mr. Sutton's class, I came across some information about ducks. Like how water beaded up and rolled off their feathers, and, because of this, the phrase "like water off a duck's back" is commonly used to refer to things that didn't bother people—how it rolls off them "like water off a duck's back." That was definitely Chloë.

Chloë was so friendly and open, it made me wonder what her middle school was like when she was in California.

Because the sense I got from the short time I'd been here at Rosecreek was that middle school would squash any "friendly and open" tendencies we might have had.

Turns out I was right.

Without a word, Chloë handed her notebook to me—the one she was carrying at recess when we became friends. The one that she doodled in sometimes. The one she hadn't shared with me until today.

It was beautiful—its edges had a metallic sheen, and a tapestry of autumn trees adorned the cover. Bits of gold sparkled among the leaves. Even the girls who acted like they didn't care about anything had eyed Chloë's notebook with envy. That's the thing. Her notebook was one of the things that made Chloë different.

And if there's one thing bullies like Miasma and Scat do, it's picking on anyone who shows a weakness or who was different in any way.

Chloë hadn't opened her French horn case yet. Instead, it was on her lap, and she was using it to rest her head. She still hadn't said anything. I decided if she handed her notebook to me, then there was something inside she wanted me to see. So, I flipped to the first page—and *wow*! Chloë was a really good artist! She'd drawn pictures of flowers, animals, abstract designs, and doodles that looked like real art, not just something scribbled like I would have done. There were three friendly elephants all walking in a line according to their height, a rainbow trout leaping over a rainbow, and dandelion-puff ladies. Really cute!

As I leafed through the notebook, there were tons of sketches of her dog, Kiko. Kiko smiling, Kiko napping, Kiko with . . . a big, huge BUTT? Kiko definitely had a fuzz-butt, but not like the ones in these sketches. Crude circles drawn together and scribbled over the carefully, lovingly sketched drawings of her dog. There was even one where Kiko had a butt for his face. It couldn't have been Chloë who did this— she would never!

I turned the page and there were more and more and more butts. Butt people with top hats, butt cats and butt fish. Page after page, every sketch of Chloë's had been butt-ified.

When Ms. Delgado emerged from the practice room, I slammed the notebook shut. Everyone looked up when she announced, "All right, class. I'm going to call you in when I'm ready for you. To keep things moving, I'm also going to ask the next pair up to sit in these chairs"—Ms. Delgado pointed to seats near her office door—"and do one last run-through while I'm grading the students ahead of you. You all have to be efficient if we're to finish today, okay?"

At this point, Ms. Delgado zeroed in on Chloë, who still hadn't opened her instrument case. I tried to get the teacher's attention and to shake my head at her, anything to signal that she should leave Chloë alone. She didn't see me, though. Instead, she clapped twice and said, "Chloë, why don't you have your horn out? Come on, now, chop-chop!"

Reluctantly, slowly, miserably, Chloë lifted her head.

Since the other students were busy getting their music and instruments ready, Ms. Delgado was hopefully the only other person to see how devastated Chloë was. Because it's one thing to feel awful, and a completely worse thing for everyone else to see it, too. Ms. Delgado's expression shifted from impatient to concerned, and without another word, she lifted the restroom pass from its hook by the door. She handed it to Chloë as she called the first group to her office. "Aileen, Tai—come on back. Kogen, Leo—you're next!"

Chloë got up like a zombie and shuffled out of the classroom.

I gripped my piccolo as hard as I could. I knew with all my heart that Miasma and Scat were behind this, but how could I prove it?

"And, class, one last thing before we start. A few of you have asked about grading for this test. You'll receive two scores." Ms. Delgado drew two overlapping circles on the whiteboard—a Venn diagram—but that's not what Miasma and Scat called it.

Snickers and laughs three rows behind me made me realize I wasn't the only one not concentrating on my music.

"Butt," chortled Miasma.

"Butt diagram," coughed Scat.

Ms. Delgado didn't turn around at all, but she did erase the circles and drew two overlapping squares instead.

"Heh-heh . . . square butt," they mumbled.

Ms. Delgado tuned them out and continued. "So, you'll

each receive an individual grade." She pointed to the two outside edges of the diagram. "And a combined grade." She pointed to the overlapping section. "Tests like this one will also prepare you for the special ensemble audition for our California trip. Remember, if you make the small group, it's free!"

Scat raised his hand. "What if we're going on the trip since our parents have already paid for it because they're rich?"

Miasma snorted and gave Scat a fist bump.

"These duet tests still factor into the progress reports, which I'll send next week," Ms. Delgado responded curtly. "And remember, not all of us have that luxury."

Anger bubbled inside me from my chest to my face. My blood rushed to my cheeks and then even my ears started to burn. Rage and frustration about the trip I undoubtedly would not be allowed to go on. Fury at Miasma and Scat for defacing Chloë's drawings.

I want them to pay, I fumed. *There need to be consequences!*

Even though I was angry on Chloë's behalf, when she walked back in the room a few minutes later, *she* looked like she had recovered completely. She was as cool and collected as the calm before a storm.

I tried to catch her eye as I adjusted my music stand. When I did, she gave me a mischievous little grin. Her eyes glowed in a way that reminded me of . . .

I gasped so loudly that several of my classmates looked up. That wasn't Chloë—it was the Amanjaku!

I fake-coughed to cover up my surprise. New Chloë just took her French horn from its case and asked me, "Shall we practice a bit?"

I gulped and nodded. How would we sound? Did the Amanjaku even know how to play?

It turned out I didn't need to worry. New Chloë was just as musical as Real Chloë. Well, almost. The new one was a bit mechanical and didn't play with the same emotion and flair that my real friend did. But she was still better than I was.

When Ms. Delgado emerged from her office and testing area, she ushered Kogen and Leo in. "Hunter and Jay, you're next!" she hollered.

As Miasma and Scat lumbered and laughed their way over to the waiting area, New Chloë pointed at a section in our duet. "Let's play this part again," she suggested sweetly. "You're going to need to do better if you want to be part of the trip's special ensemble."

"There's no way," I muttered as I raised my piccolo to my lips. "You know I won't be allowed to go."

"Do I?" New Chloë arched an eyebrow at me. "Do you *wish* to go? Because I can make that happen, if that is something you truly want. . . ."

"Of course I *want* it." I paused to blow the starting note into my piccolo. "I want a lot of things, but I don't see how you can help, especially since—"

"You're flat," giggled New Chloë. "Let's try again, okay?"

Instead of explaining what she meant by saying "I can make that happen," New Chloë insisted we practice the same section over and over again. After a few more run-throughs, we sounded better, but not by a lot.

New Chloë scolded, "You don't practice a whole lot, do you?"

"You sound like my mother," I grumbled. She looked hurt.

Ms. Delgado emerged from her office again and looked our way. "All good?" she asked.

New Chloë's expression changed when she turned to our teacher. "Much better, thank you!"

"All right, then. You and Melony are after Hunter and Jay."

With that, Miasma and Scat went to play their duet with Ms. Delgado as New Chloë and I took our seats outside her office. I set our music on the stand and prepared to play our piece once more, but New Chloë had other plans. From the bell of her French horn, she pulled out two silver Sharpies and handed me one.

"What's this for?" I asked.

New Chloë looked around and I followed her gaze. Almost everyone was busy getting ready for their duet exam. Miasma and Scat were commanding Ms. Delgado's full attention. There were a few kids goofing off, but they weren't paying any attention to us.

New Chloë drew one circle, then another on her music

stand. The silver butt drawing stood out like a double moon against the black metal.

My jaw dropped. "What do you think you're doing?" I whispered as quietly but insistently as I could.

"Quick." She looked around again to make sure no one was watching. "Do your stand, too, and then cover it with your music."

"What? No!" I said more loudly than I meant to. Even though the band office and testing area was soundproof, I could swear I saw Ms. Delgado look our way. Chloë brought her horn up to her mouth and muttered to me instead of playing. "Look, you gotta do it too, or both those boys won't get in trouble. You wanted there to be *consequences*, right?"

I did, but . . . I hadn't *told* anyone that! How did she know? But I thought again about how Miasma and Scat had ruined my friend's beautiful drawings, about how the real Chloë was probably still crying in the bathroom, and how I wanted the boys to pay for what they'd done. . . .

Could the Amanjaku come and go as it pleased? Or was it because I wished it? Was that why the Amanjaku was here and not Chloë? Not the *real* Chloë, anyway.

"Come on," she hissed. "We're running out of time."

As quickly as I could, I drew butt after butt on the music stand. When I was finished, New Chloë stood up like something had stung her.

"Ms. Delgado," she blurted out as our band teacher

emerged from the practice room with Miasma and Scat.

"What is it, Chloë?" she asked. Her brow furrowed with concern.

"Umm . . . I know you want the duets to move efficiently today, but—" New Chloë went pale and pointed at the drawings on her music stand.

"Heh-heh," Scat giggled. "She said 'butt.'"

The blood drained from Ms. Delgado's face, too, when she saw what the boys had drawn. Only they hadn't drawn anything. New Chloë and I had done all of it, but no one knew that but us. "They're on Melony's stand too."

I gulped and moved my music out of the way so Ms. Delgado could see.

"Oh, Ms. Delgado, this is so upsetting." New Chloë wrung her hands and blinked her eyes like she was about to cry. "We can't possibly play well today. We're too upset."

We are? I thought. New Chloë locked eyes with me for the briefest of moments. *We are!* I blinked too and fake-wiped a nonexistent tear away.

Ms. Delgado's ears went from pale to bright red.

"I completely understand," she muttered through her clenched teeth. "Hunter. Jay. In the hall. We need to have a little talk."

When the bell rang at the end of class, I followed New Chloë down the hallway. She strode with confidence into the bathroom. I paused for a moment before going in after her. But when I did, I almost ran into Real Chloë, who was patting her face dry with a paper towel.

"Are you okay?" I asked my friend.

"I think I am now," Chloë responded. "Sorry about stranding you in band class. Did we miss our duet?"

"No, um . . ." I tried to scan the bathroom out of the corner of my eye for the other Chloë. "Things didn't exactly go as efficiently as Ms. Delgado wanted," I explained as I wondered where the Amanjaku disappeared to.

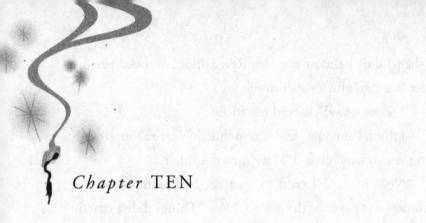

Chapter TEN

"Suspended?!" Chloë squealed.

Hearing that Miasma and Scat got what was coming to them didn't undo their damage to Chloë's notebook. But it certainly helped her feel a little better.

"It's only in-school," I explained. "But at least it means we're free of them for three whole days!"

Chloë frowned. "That seems like a lot."

Wait, was she feeling *sorry* for them? After what they did to her? She should be annoyed that it wasn't more!

"But they're always doing bad things, even before today," I grumbled. "It really is their fault."

"Yeah, everything adds up." Chloë nodded slowly. "And what were they thinking? Drawing on the music stands with Sharpies, sheesh!"

"I know, right?" A twinge of guilt hit me out of the blue. After all, they ruined my friend's notebook, the one that her best friend had given her. Plus, it was from France, so it's not like she could have gotten a new one very easily. But my stomach still flipped a little when I let her think that Miasma and Scat had drawn on the stands and not me and the Amanjaku.

"Uriko, do you want to go shopping this weekend?" Back at home, my mom acted like she was in a good mood, but I knew what was up. The night after the Amanjaku arrived, I'd overheard my parents talking.

"Do you see how much better she is now that we've given her some space?" Dad asked.

"I think she was just tired the other night," my mom responded. "She would have been worse if we *had* let her go to that sleepover."

"Still," my dad whispered. "Maybe we should let her have some more fun."

"She has way more fun than I ever did at her age!" my mom argued. "She has plenty. She's gotten to play with Chloë-chan a couple times and . . ." At this point, my mom paused.

"And?" my dad prompted.

". . . school," Mom added. But even *she* didn't sound convinced that this was a great example.

"I am telling you," my dad muttered in a way that sounded regretful, "it's like trying to pack an already-full suitcase. If you try to put too much in and latch it closed, it will just end up exploding on you."

So my dad was saying I was a suitcase? And I was going to explode? But then why was my mom offering to buy me more clothes if the suitcase was already so full? Sometimes parents made no sense.

Turns out my mom just wanted to go shopping to pick up more fabric scraps for her quilting. Since I'd also been bugging her about letting me spend the twenty-four dollars they'd given me for my birthday, it was a "kill two birds with one stone" type of errand. Even so, my middle school wardrobe definitely could've used some help. Not because I'd actually grown out of a lot of my clothes from elementary school, but because I didn't want to be known as the outdated fashion nightmare of Rosecreek Middle School.

First, we stopped for ice cream. It was chilly outside but that didn't matter to a die-hard ice cream fan like me. Even though my mom normally didn't eat a ton of regular ice cream and the chocolate or cookies-and-cream flavors so many people were drawn to, she did like this particular shop with its specialty flavors. It served a persimmon sorbet—my mom's favorite. It was a deep orange hue with a hint of cinnamon flavor. She let me try the tiniest of spoonfuls once and it reminded me of carrot cake and pumpkin pie, only it was more refreshing and not as sweet. It was the only flavor she ever bought.

Even though this was a super-popular shop, the colder weather meant a shorter line. Not a bad way to start out. Not at all! Then Mom let me order a waffle cone. She hardly ever did that because, "Sugar cones are just like waffle cones and you don't need to pay more for them."

But today was different. So, I ordered a regular single scoop—not a kid-sized one—of watermelon chip. Maybe Dad had convinced her that was one of the perks of turning twelve. The scooper was extra generous, too, as he packed the deep pink ice cream down to the very bottom of the cone as well.

"Melony eating watermelon ice cream?" My mom's eyes widened. "Isn't that a bit like cannibalism?" I liked the persimmon sorbet as much as she did, but I didn't want to have the same thing like we were twinsies. I regretted my decision a little, though, when she made this comment.

"Ha ha." I granted my mom a laugh even though her joke wasn't very amusing. People always complain about dad jokes, but let me tell you—mom jokes are pretty bad too. Since she *did* just buy me ice cream, I held back telling her that she's told that one before (and it wasn't funny the first three times either).

But then Mom went back to being Mom when I started to stroll down the street to peek in the windows of all the shops.

"Melony? What are you doing? Come back and sit with me."

I licked my ice cream and nibbled on the crunchy cone as I walked back toward her.

"But don't walk while you're eating."

I stopped. "You just told me to come back." I bristled.

"Yes, come back, but wait to eat until you're sitting. It's rude."

Mom was always like this with ice cream. I'd assumed she was worried it would fall off its cone and then we'd have wasted a bunch of money. But I never realized it was because she thought I had bad ice cream manners.

I pulled a rickety metal chair out from the table in front of the shop and flounced down. "How's it rude?" I asked as I caught a melting drip with my tongue. I looked around at the other cold-weather ice cream lovers who were walking around while enjoying their cones.

"In Japan," my mother explained, "most people don't walk around while they eat. What if you were to bump into someone?"

"There's barely anyone here." I tried to keep the edge out of my voice, but I think it still came through.

"Still." My mom sniffed.

Despite the fact that I was sitting on a cold metal chair in frosty weather, eating an icy treat with a chilly silence extending between us, I began to feel warm. A spark of anger igniting and urging me to retort, *But we're not in Japan*.

I took another bite and concentrated on the sweet chocolate chip "seeds" mingling with the refreshing watermelon flavor. It took my mind off being stuck in my chair. At being held in check.

Maybe the rest of the afternoon will be better, I thought.

It wasn't.

* * *

The Red, White, and Blue is the local thrift store we love to go to. It's massive and filled to the brim with tons of clothes *and* random things like plates, books, fabric, and jewelry. I could spend hours there.

Don't get me wrong, I liked going to fancy shopping centers and looking at new things, but it's not real shopping where you can actually afford stuff. It's more like "wishful shopping" where I checked the price tags on anything I liked. But with that, I usually just ended up depressed. How could I ever convince my mom to spend fifty dollars on a new dress when I could get it for five dollars at the Red, White, and Blue? So that's why I liked this place. As long as you were willing to put in the time, you could find almost anything here, and for a *steal*.

I inhaled deeply as we entered the Red, White, and Blue. It always smelled kind of funny. Maybe a little bit like a garage or an attic? A bit old, a hint of must. Almost like a tired sigh. But above all, it smelled like undiscovered treasure.

Unlike the department store, where the clothes were organized by designer, at the thrift store, they were organized in categories like "Pants," "Dresses," and "Shirts." And then everything was organized by color. It was much easier to find things I wanted than wondering, *Hmm . . . Will the Gucci section have a shirt I'd like today? No? Guess I'll have to go check another-fancy-brand-I-could-never-in-my-wildest-dreams-afford.*

Since it was a Saturday *and* there was a sale, the store was teeming with other shoppers eager to find a bargain, so I grabbed a basket. That's the one thing about the Red, White, and Blue—if you weren't on your toes, someone else would find your treasure before you could!

I first headed toward the "Pants" section. Then, I walked down the aisle until I came to a long rack of just jeans. There were jeans with elastic waists (the type of jeans I saw old ladies wearing), skinny jeans (the type I saw a lot of the moms wearing), and then *the coolest* ripped jeans. They had my size, so I threw them in my basket.

Then I looked through the shirts. There was a sweatshirt that was black and super baggy. I loved it! I tossed that one in along with another shirt with neat holes in it. Not holes from being old and worn, but *designer* holes, all slashed on one shoulder in parallel lines, like a tiger took one swipe at it with its claws. There was a girl at school who had one just like it—only it was pink and not green like the one here. The girl herself was mean, even to her so-called friends, but I *did* think her shirt was cool.

"Have you found some things you want?" my mom asked.

"Maybe," I responded. I don't know why I didn't say "Yes!" or why I turned my body so she couldn't see into my basket easily.

"Is *that* what you picked out?"

Oh yeah, that's *why.*

Mom took a step toward me, and before I could stop her, she'd already fished out the baggy black sweatshirt. She held it up against me and made a face. "This is too big for you, isn't it? And such a gloomy style! You look so much nicer in bright colors."

I tried to move my basket out of arm's reach, but my mom didn't get the hint.

"Ugh! These jeans are ripped. And this shirt's a pretty color but filled with holes!" My mom held the green tiger-slashed shirt away from her like it was filthy.

"It's only a dollar fifty," I muttered, even though I knew the low price wouldn't make a difference.

"Of course it is!" my mom replied, exactly how I knew she would. "It's all torn up! Did you want me to mend it? I can fix a lot of things, but it would be very difficult to make this look nice and neat."

"It doesn't *need* fixing, Mom! This is the style."

My mom made a face. "Really? So it's like this on purpose? Wow. Girls your age wouldn't be allowed to wear anything like that in Japan." She rummaged through her own basket. "What about this?" My mom held up a button-down collared shirt. It was cream-colored with a delicate embroidered pattern in white on its two front pockets. It reminded me of a lace tablecloth, the kind you might find at your grandma's house.

I wouldn't be caught *dead* in that. Wait, I take that back.

It would be the perfect shirt for me to wear in my coffin to indicate that there was no more life—in not only my body, but my soul.

"What do you think, Uri-chan? This embroidery was done by hand, and whoever did it was very skilled. You don't see handiwork like this very often!" My mom checked the price tag. "It's only three dollars, so you'd still have twenty-one dollars left of your birthday money. Kawaii deshou?"

Kawaii? My mom should know that I wasn't into being "kawaii." Elementary school kids might be into being cute, but not middle schoolers. At least, not this one. But I nodded because she clearly wanted me to get this, whether I liked it or not.

Last year, I'd really enjoyed coming here with my mom. But this time, I left everything I wanted at the store and couldn't wait for this shopping trip to be over.

Chapter ELEVEN

J ust when I was feeling stuck in a rut in my life, Chloë saved the day. The *real* Chloë.

"Are you coming to the PTA meeting tonight?" Chloë whispered to me near the end of Mr. Sutton's class on Wednesday.

"Why would I do that?" I whispered back as I watched the Dread Pirate R take two hops to the end of his cage, turn, and hop back.

"Because I'm going." Chloë giggled like she had a secret she could barely contain. "And so are your parents."

"What?" I said loudly enough that Mr. Sutton turned around from the whiteboard.

He silenced us with a stern look.

After class, Chloë filled me in as quickly as she could. "I told my mom about the school band trip and how you hadn't asked your parents yet because you were sure they'd say no.

So, my mom called yours today and she said—"

At that moment a *honk* directed my attention toward my dad's waiting car. While I appreciated that they were always on time, today I wished they were a couple minutes late.

"You'll see!" Chloë waved at me as she ran to her bus.

"Melony-chan, why didn't you tell us about the band trip?" my dad immediately chided me as I buckled my seat belt.

"I figured you would have said no," I sulked. But then I sat up with a hope beyond hopes. "*Will* you let me go?"

"Hmm," my dad responded as he stopped at the intersection near the school. "We haven't decided for sure yet."

At home, my mother fretted about her outfit for the meeting I still couldn't believe we were going to. "What you have on is fine!" I reassured my mom. Remembering the beautiful scarf that Mrs. Yoshida was wearing the first time I met her, I looked inside my mom's closet. I pulled out a blue-green silk wrap that was the color of peacock feathers.

"This would look nice with your sweater," I said as I handed it to her.

My mom draped it loosely around her shoulders. "Thank you, Uri-chan," she said as she fixed her hair in her bedroom mirror.

"You're welcome," I responded in my sweetest voice. I didn't even point out to her that her sweater was black, just like the "gloomy" sweatshirt she didn't want me to buy from the thrift store. I *so* wanted to go on this trip!

My dad, meanwhile, was reading the information packet. He underlined certain sections and also scribbled questions in a notebook.

At the meeting, I watched as my parents scanned the room for a place to sit. Luckily, Mr. and Mrs. Yoshida were already there and had saved them seats.

"Kids, we have a project you can help with in the commons," the PTA president said, and directed us out of the cafeteria.

Out in the school entryway, Chloë and I worked on assembling lollipops and attaching cards with the names of the kids they would go to. For a couple dollars, our classmates ordered these candies that class representatives would deliver to their friends. The cards didn't say who they were from, only who they were going to.

"What do you think they're talking about?" I paused to look toward where the meeting had been going on for over an hour now.

"My mom said it was all the groups that needed fundraising, including band. The PTA is discussing how money will be divided," Chloë answered as she attached a card to a lollipop with a ribbon.

"No, I mean them." I used a lollipop to point to our parents whispering to each other in the back row.

Chloë joined me in looking through the window. "Just making sure you'll get to go on the trip!"

"How can you be so sure?" I asked. They were still talking,

and I wanted so badly to hear what they were saying.

"Because it's something I wished for more than anything," Chloë said as she finished preparing another lollipop. She pulled another card from the box.

"Hey!" she exclaimed. "This one's for me!"

I grinned. "It's the worst when you don't get any, so I bought you one," I confessed, even though I wanted it to be a surprise on the day the candy was distributed.

Chloë laughed. "I know. We had the same type of thing at my old school in California." She pointed to the next card, which had my name on it.

I pulled that card from the box. "You got me one too?"

"Of course!" Chloë responded. "But it looks like I'm not the only one."

Sure enough, the last card in the box had my name on it too. It reminded me of the handwriting that was on the package that the Amanjaku arrived in.

My heart skipped a beat, and not in a good way. A shiver ran through me.

". . . Miasma?" Chloë asked. She looked at me like she could hardly believe it herself. "It *would* explain why he plays the piccolo—"

"Eww, gross!" That thought had never crossed my mind before. Now I felt nauseous. I grabbed the card with my name on it and crumpled it up.

"Ready to go, girls?" Mrs. Yoshida appeared behind us. "We just finished. Are you almost done?"

Chloë jumped up and hugged her mom. "Were you able to get them to—?"

"Agree to let Melony go on the band trip?" My mom finished Chloë's sentence for her as she and my dad joined us. The other parents milled past them on their way out.

"Yes!" my dad responded. "At first, we were absolutely against it. Three nights away is a long time!"

"But then Mrs. Yoshida reminded us about shuugaku ryokou," my mom added. "The overnight trip that Japanese sixth graders take with their class."

"I learned about it in a Japanese culture and society class in college," Mrs. Yoshida explained as she gave me a sly wink that my parents didn't see.

I inhaled quickly and held my breath. *Could it be that they'll actually let me go?*

"But taking a flight to California—" My dad shook his head.

My hope began to leave me like air from a leaky tire.

"Then the Yoshidas said they were going to chaperone, so . . ." My mom traded looks with my father.

I waited for what seemed like an eternity. *So . . . ?*

"We decided that you could go. Maybe."

I was about to exhale with relief until I heard the last word. *Maybe what?*

"Some conditions will need to be met," my mom clarified. "Melony, you're going to have to be very, very good."

Chapter TWELVE

could hardly believe it. This wish of mine, this wish for freedom and adventure, was so close to coming true! And the Amanjaku wasn't the one who granted it. It was because of my good friend—my *best* friend—Chloë and her parents.

But it turns out that being good is hard work. After the PTA meeting, my parents outlined what I'd need to do to earn my spot on the spring break band trip.

You have to help out more around the house.

I had chores before, but I have to admit, I didn't always do them. And even when I did, I sometimes (okay, maybe often) didn't do them well. I had to empty the dishwasher in the mornings, but on weekends when I slept until noon, one of my parents would just do it because they got tired of waiting for me. I was supposed to fold and put away my laundry every day, but I always felt my outfits were easier to put together when my clothes were spread out on my floor. We had two bathrooms in the house: one off my parents' bedroom and another one in the hallway that I used. If we had guests, they would have used mine too, but since we hardly ever did, I let mine get pretty gross on occasion. My mom often got after me to clean it, but I used my homework as an excuse as to why I couldn't do it right away. So, the bathroom would stay messy, or my mom would just end up doing it.

Not anymore, though. I accomplished all of the above and then some.

You can only go on the trip if you keep your grades up.

Truth is, I wasn't the type of student to do extra work. Several of my teachers offered us opportunities to retake tests or quizzes or to correct our answers and turn them in for half credit. But I never did that . . . until now. In addition to convincing my parents to let me go on the band trip, the Yoshidas also taught my parents how to access the school's parent-student portal through which they could log in and see my grades. My parents weren't very tech-savvy, so I never bothered to teach them how to use it, thinking that they'd only get frustrated with it. But now that Chloë's parents had walked them through it, they checked my grades several times a week!

And even though today was a Sunday, I worked on the owl report I was writing for Mr. Sutton's class. It wasn't all bad, though. I learned interesting facts, like how owls can't really turn their heads all the way around—only three-quarters of the way. And that they couldn't get rabies!

You can only go on the trip if you make the special ensemble.

This hurdle was going to be the hardest one for me. Even though there were only two piccolo players, there was no way both of us were going to be chosen for the ensemble. There's a joke that Ms. Delgado told us at the beginning of the year that asks, "How do you tune two piccolos?" The answer? "You get rid of one of them." She thought it was hilarious, but it definitely didn't help me feel any better about having to sit next to Miasma the whole year. Despite being a general disaster in other ways, my nemesis was surprisingly good at the piccolo, and since I hardly ever practiced . . .

"Why do I have to make the ensemble in order to go on the trip?" I whined when my mom outlined this final term for me. "If I don't, I know the trip won't be free, but there will be fundraisers to help the rest of the band members afford—"

"But not enough. For us, anyway," my mom answered in a matter-of-fact way. "And besides, I know you will be chosen if you try your best."

After doing almost everything I needed to this weekend, I was pretty exhausted by Sunday afternoon. I had spent over an hour trying to master a particularly tough section of music that had a tricky rhythm followed by a scale made up of sixteenth notes.

After that, I was in the process of putting away my laundry when I held up the new shirt my mom made me buy at the Red, White, and Blue. Freshly laundered ("Because you can never be too careful with items that have been used," as my mom said) and ironed, sure, it looked like it was worth more than the three dollars spent on it. Still, that didn't mean I liked it. I resisted the urge to crumple it up and bury it at the bottom of one of my dresser drawers. *They'll let me go on the trip if I'm good*, I reminded myself. I carefully hung it up in the back of my closet and slid the door closed.

But how cool would I have looked in that green shirt? The memory of the clothes I left behind popped into my head. If I had bought it, I could have paired it with the ripped jeans, which would also go with the baggy black sweatshirt—worn off the shoulder with a red tank top underneath. Those would definitely be cool outfits!

But I didn't have any of these items, so what use was it to think about them? Before I could stop myself, I wished I could go shopping *without* my mom. I wished that I could buy the clothes that *I* wanted. Without judgment, my mom's raised eyebrows, or disapproving comments.

I pulled back the curtains to my window—lace curtains that very much resembled the shirt I'd just hidden away and would never wear. Outside, the persimmons were ripening on our old neighbor's tree. It had shed most of its leaves by this point, but its deep orange fruit hung on, refusing to let go. One of the tree's branches hung above our fence and dangled an orange orb over our yard. I could tell that even on my tiptoes it would be just out of reach.

Like so many things in your life.

Just then, the doorbell rang.

"Hi, Mrs. Yoshimura. I was biking by and just thought I'd check and see if Melony could play."

I forgot all about the neighbor's persimmons when I heard Chloë's voice. What was *she* doing here? At recess on Friday, she'd mentioned that she'd be busy this weekend because her family had guests visiting from California. I was a little jealous because I wondered if she'd be hanging out with a friend from the school she used to go to, but she didn't say anything about it, so I didn't ask.

I ran down the hall, where my mom and Chloë were talking by the front door. She was wearing a glittering purple bike helmet.

"Uriko, did you finish all your chores?" my mom asked.

"Um . . . not completely." I looked down, not wanting to meet my mom's eyes. There wasn't anything on our Sunday schedule, so I had been putting off gathering the trash from the different rooms.

"Oh, that's too bad." Chloë lowered her eyes too. "I was hoping you could bike to the store with me. I guess I'll go home, then. Mom won't let me go by myself."

"Hmm," my mom muttered. She scanned our neighborhood surroundings as if making sure there were no monsters waiting to ambush us. Finally, she responded, "I agree with your mother, Chloë-chan. Going by yourself wouldn't be a good idea. But I do remember in Japan children your age would bike places together. Uriko? If you promise to finish your last chore as soon as you return—before five, please—you can go play with your friend."

Yes! I couldn't believe it. My mom hadn't let me bike to the store ever since Louisa moved away. "I'll just go grab my wallet!" I hollered as I ran down the hallway to my room.

"And your helmet!" my mom called out after me.

"Ittekimasu!" I shouted goodbye to my mom in Japanese, which I hardly ever did in front of people outside of my family. But Chloë had said she thought it was cool, *plus* it always made my parents happy when I did. Since they were letting me go, I didn't mind being nice back.

"Be careful!" my mom shouted after us. "Let me know when you get to the store!"

Since she said this in English, clearly she meant for Chloë to listen too. "And when you're headed back, too. Watch for traffic at that intersection at Welling and Oak River! You know cars take that turn without looking, and make sure to . . ."

My mom's voice was drowned out by the rumbling and squeaking of the garage door. As soon as I retrieved my bike, I pedaled away like we were being chased. After all, I didn't want my mom to change her mind . . . or to give us any more directions! I was *so* thankful that Chloë had arrived to save me from certain boredom, but something tickled at the back of my mind. Something about the way she asked my mom if I could "play" when my mom answered the door. I know that's what my mom called it, but no middle schooler called it that. The last time someone wanted to "play" was . . . the Amanjaku!

But *I* was able to tell the difference between Real Chloë and the Amanjaku. I noticed right away, the first time we hung out, that the Amanjaku's voice was more hollow, almost like an echo of Real Chloë's voice. When the Amanjaku helped trick Miasma and Scat into getting in-school suspension, its eyes glowed. But the person who came to my door? It was the real Chloë, it had to be!

As we biked the back trails to avoid the traffic on the main road, I forgot my doubts for a moment as the wind *whooshed* past my face. What a feeling it was, to be free! Out from the walls of my house and on an adventure with a friend. No adults!

An owl fluttering past caught my eye. "Who, who, who, whoooo?" It hooted just like Bob did, with its barred-owl call. "Who, who, who, whoooo?"

I thudded through a pothole when the owl swooped close to my head and then landed in the trees bordering our path. It stared at me like it knew me, and I briefly wondered if it was Bob from our backyard. But that seemed silly, because why would he be so far from the woods where he normally was?

Chloë didn't seem to notice at all, though, as she chattered about how overprotective her mom was for not letting her bike alone and that she was glad I was home because it was more fun to bike with me anyway.

It sure sounds like Chloë, I thought. But something about

the way the owl sounded—almost like it was urging me to question who I was with—made me decide to test her.

"Hey, I thought you had visitors from . . . New York," I called out to her. "What are they doing now?"

"Oh, they're awful." Chloë giggled. "We had pizza last night and they went on and on about how it was probably pretty good for Oregon pizza, but New York–style pizza was the best. Rude, right? And they *demanded* bagels and lox for breakfast and New York–style cheesecake for dessert."

A lot of people think New York is famous for pizza, bagels, and cheesecake, but I met someone from Brooklyn a few years ago and she didn't mention a word about these things even once. These New Yorkers at Chloë's house sounded weirdly obsessed with food. In fact, it made me think of the first time the Amanjaku visited and couldn't get enough of the hot chocolate, cookies, and chips I served. . . .

I skidded to a stop. "I thought your guests were from California."

Chloë slowed down and paused too. We were underneath a bridge and the cars roared as they drove above us. A bead of sweat trickled down my back, and I shivered even though I was warm from our bike ride.

When she turned around, she tightened the strap under her chin without a word. Her eyes glinted—hard, like the glittering purple of her helmet—in the shadow of the bridge.

"Ha! I knew something was up." Even though my tone was light, I looked around hoping that we weren't the only two people on this lonely, dusty trail.

"But how?" the Amanjaku finally replied, sounding genuinely disappointed. "I've been working on my voice. Don't I sound just like her?"

She did, still, even though I had busted the Amanjaku's cover. "You were a little overly specific in your lie," I explained before I could decide whether I should have or not. "Details are good, but when I caught you, there was no way to backtrack and explain you were actually talking about your guests from California."

New Chloë nodded, taking in this new information. "I see. Thank you." Her eyes had returned to Chloë's soft brown shade. So much so that I almost believed it was really her again.

"Well, do you still want to go to the store with me?" the Amanjaku asked. "I got the sense that's what you wanted to do. Plus, I've never gone shopping for clothes, and I'd like to know what that's like."

Part of me knew I should go home right away. But another part couldn't stop thinking about the clothes *I* wanted that I couldn't buy with my mom. I mean, I guess I could have, but she was so critical that all the joy of having them would have been sucked out.

"I still have to be back by five," I grumbled. As if she knew I was going to answer that way, Chloë had already started biking down the trail, and I had to pedal hard to catch up.

Back at the Red, White, and Blue, New Chloë looked over my shoulder as I sent a text to my mom from my ridiculous phone: "We have managed to arrive without being kidnapped or run over by a truck." My friend snickered, but I backspaced and deleted everything after the word "arrive."

"Why'd you erase that?" New Chloë asked.

I shrugged. "I don't think my mom would appreciate the sarcasm."

Then New Chloë took a basket when I took a basket. She didn't search through the same clothes I went through, but I could feel her watching me from an aisle away and rifling through the clothes on the racks behind me, just as I was doing.

"It's still here!" I gasped as I found the slashed green shirt I had eyed last time. New Chloë appeared by my side with her own pile of clothes.

"That shirt would look *so good* on you!" she chirped. "Those rips are *so cool*. And it's a great color."

"It is, isn't it?" I beamed. I was already having way more fun than when I was here with my mom. "What did you find?"

New Chloë put down her basket and held up *my baggy black sweatshirt and ripped jeans*! Although, I guess they weren't mine, technically, but I had planned to look for them next. New Chloë had found them, though, so it wasn't like I could tell her she couldn't have them, but . . .

"These would look great on you, don't you think?" New

Chloë took the black sweatshirt out and held it up toward me. "The size is perfect, and with a red tank top underneath, you'd look *very* stylish."

"Uh, thanks." I was really happy she'd found it for me, but I was still pretty unnerved that somehow she knew exactly what I wanted.

"Here, hold it up against yourself," New Chloë ordered.

I did as I was told as my friend fished out her phone from a zippered pocket.

Her phone! I had wondered where it had disappeared to after the first time we met. But before I could ask about it, New Chloë tossed some clothes at my face.

"And these jeans! They cost *way* more at department stores, you know." I held the pants against myself as I checked the length. New Chloë took another photo.

"Look!" New Chloë showed me her phone. On it was a picture of me wearing a complete outfit, baggy black sweatshirt and ripped jeans all together.

"How'd you do that?" I asked. I took her phone from her and looked closer. I really *did* look cool!

"It's just an app," New Chloë informed me like it wasn't amazing at all.

I was really falling behind the times with my parents' refusal to get me a real phone!

"Aren't you going to get anything?" I asked New Chloë to mask my embarrassment about not knowing anything about fun technology.

New Chloë shrugged. "What would I do with them?" she asked.

"Oh yeah." It was easy to forget that this wasn't really Chloë in front of me.

Remembering that made me want to return home all of a sudden. "I'll check out and meet you up front, okay?"

"Wait!" It turned out that New Chloë had one more item in her basket. A pair of boots—the kind all the girls had at school, but were *way* too expensive, especially considering that I was still growing. At least that's what my mom always said.

"These would fit you, right?"

I slipped on the soft fleece-lined boots, and it felt like clouds were wrapped around my feet. There was even a bit of wiggle room around the toes.

"They're perfect," I sighed. But when I checked out the price, *that* certainly wasn't.

If I bought the jeans, the green shirt, and the sweatshirt, that brought me to ten dollars. Factoring in the three bucks I used to buy the lace-doily shirt my mom recommended, that brought me to thirteen of my twenty-four dollars of birthday money. Unfortunately, the boots were twelve dollars, which was a pretty hefty price for this particular store, but they looked new, so I understood why.

Darn it! If my mom hadn't guilted me into spending money on something *she* liked, I would have had enough money. I slipped them off and handed them back to Chloë.

"They're really nice, but I would need another dollar," I explained. "Thanks for showing me, though."

I stood in line while the Amanjaku returned the boots to the shelf where it had found them.

As I began to remove the hangers on my other items for the woman at the register, New Chloë came bounding up with the boots.

"She'll take these too!" she chirped to the checker.

"Chloë!" I snapped. "I told you I can't afford them—"

"You know blue tags are thirty percent off today, right?" The cashier punched the discounted price into her register.

Blue tags? I could have sworn the boots had a red sticker on them when I looked at the price, moments ago. Every day, the Red, White, and Blue had a special discount on one of its tag colors. Usually, it was on items that had been there too long. But I was a pro shopping here, and I *knew*—or at least I was 99 percent sure—that the price was printed on red just a few minutes before.

"Sorry." New Chloë looked very contrite. "Do you want me to put them back? It just seemed like you really wanted them."

Now *I* felt bad for making *her* feel bad. "No, I mean, I didn't realize they were discounted today."

"Yeah, these look practically new." The checker frowned as she examined the barely scuffed soles. "I'm surprised they're discounted too. Oh well, this is your lucky day! If you'd still like them, that is."

It wasn't a matter of liking them. I loved them! But that sticker was red before, I was almost certain. I glanced in New Chloë's direction. *Did she switch the tags?*

She wouldn't meet my gaze, though. Instead, she stared intently at her phone the way all the kids did after school when they were finally allowed to take them out of their lockers. The way they did when they didn't want to talk to anyone. Or maybe anyone like me.

I knew she did it.

"I . . ." I *wanted* to tell the cashier that she could put the boots back. But even more than that, I wanted them to be mine.

I looked around. There were three other checkers all busy helping other customers purchase piles of clothes, shoes, and other items. The place was huge and filled with *stuff*. Did my measly Amanjaku discount harm anyone in the grand scheme of things?

The cashier sighed, impatient. "Well?"

"I'll take them!" I responded in the spur of the moment. Chloë looked up from her phone and smiled. At that moment, she reminded me of how the Amanjaku looked the first day we met. When it gobbled up our cookies and looked around for more. My heart pounded for some reason then. Was I scared we'd be caught? Or was I afraid of something else—

"That'll be $8.40." The cashier interrupted my thoughts.

I emptied my wallet and handed over the bulk of what was left of my birthday money. When I snuck another peek at New Chloë, she was back to scrolling through her phone. She giggled and then held it up toward me.

It was a video of three fluffy puppies trying to walk down some stairs. The first one tripped, and then another tumbled, and the third toppled over them all. Each dog stood back up, though. No one was hurt.

This hurts no one, I convinced myself. *No one at all.*

On the bike ride home, I worried about how I was going to get my new clothes inside, especially since my mom is always super nosy about everything I buy when she's not around.

But the Amanjaku assured me it would be fine. "Just take the boots inside. She won't object to those, right? I'll find a way to get the rest of the clothes to you without her seeing."

We arrived back at my place at 4:55 p.m. Even though this was five minutes before I *had* to be back and I had texted when we left the store just like she'd asked me to, my mom was already out front, waiting.

"It's starting to get dark," my mom greeted us. "Are you going to be okay biking back to your place alone, Chloë? I'm wondering if I should drive you home."

"Don't worry! Sunset isn't until 5:45," New Chloë replied. "But thank you." Then she handed me my boots from the bag of clothes that she had agreed to take care of for me.

"Wow, those are nice!" Mom commented as I took them from Chloë.

"I thought they'd look good on Melony," New Chloë said.

"I found them, but they're still a little too big for me."

"Such a good girl." My mom gave my friend a warm smile.

Ugh. I would have been annoyed at the Amanjaku sucking up to my mom if it weren't doing it to help me.

"Thank you," New Chloë smiled back. In the approaching dusk, her teeth seemed to gleam an unnatural white.

Even though New Chloë had said she'd be fine, my mom watched her until she was almost a block away before heading back inside. But I kept my eyes on her for a few more seconds and had to keep from gasping when New Chloë, my bag of clothes, and her bike literally faded into the surrounding air.

That evening, after I'd showered and brushed and flossed my teeth, I slipped into bed . . . and as I laid my head down, under my pillow I felt the clothes that I'd bought from the store. Freshly laundered and folded. In my house.

I had no idea how the Amanjaku could have brought them in here without my knowing.

I wondered, *Has it been here other times without me knowing too?*

My heart thudded in my chest at the thought. It rattled around my rib cage and pounded so hard, it felt like it was trying to escape.

"*Pata pata pat-tan, tat-ton ton.*

Pata pata pat-tan, tat-ton ton."

My mom's gentle singing while she worked on her new quilt downstairs calmed me down.

"*Pata pata pat-tan, tat-ton ton.*

Pata pata pat-tan, tat-ton ton."

"Tadaima!" My dad was home now too.

"Okaeri." I heard my mom welcome him home. "How was work?"

"Maa, it was tiring, as usual," my dad responded. "A part on one of the machines broke, so I had to spend over an hour trying to figure out what was wrong. . . ."

Gradually, my parents' chatter made me feel safe and sleepy.

I had fun today. I breathed in. Being good enough so that my parents would allow me to go on the trip was hard work. Everyone needs a break some time, right?

I felt free. I breathed out.

A few dollars is so *not a big deal.* I breathed in.

I didn't hurt anyone. I breathed out.

Chapter THIRTEEN

"Californians." Chloë rolled her eyes in exasperation the following Tuesday afternoon at recess. "All our guests did was miss their green smoothies and complain about how cold and gray it is here."

"So, would you say you like Oregon more?" I asked as we trudged around the track like we usually did. The air was so frosty that my question came out like wisps of clouds.

"Oh yeah, one hundred percent." Chloë made her mittened hand reply to me like a sock puppet.

Definitely different, I thought. Real Chloë's grin was sincere and sweet, not like the Amanjaku when it appeared as her. The Amanjaku had me fooled this weekend with the adjustments it had made to its voice and its eyes, but its smile wasn't the same as Chloë's. It was hard to put my finger on it, but it almost felt like the Amanjaku was *acting* happy when it would smile. It was forced, or something like that. I didn't want to think about it right now, or about the several dollars I didn't pay to the Red, White, and Blue.

It didn't hurt anyone, I told myself again.

I let out a little sigh of relief when Chloë said she liked it here. Not that us kids have much influence in where our parents make us live, but I was happy to hear that the Yoshidas' visit with their old friends didn't make them miss their old home and want to move back. And with the weather like it was today, I could see how—Californian or not—it would be hard to see the charms of dreary Oregon.

This morning had felt like autumn was playing tug-of-war with winter—and losing. It was lucky for me, though, because it allowed me to wear my long winter jacket over my new outfit, which made it easy to hide it from my mom. I could also wear my new fleece-lined boots!

"Those *are* nice." My mom had commented on them when I stepped into the car. "How much were they again?"

"Only $8.40," I'd answered. Only, I don't know why I said that and not twelve. It's not like I kept the receipt or that she even knew about the other clothes. And even if she did, I doubt she'd go back to the store, calculate how much I spent, and know that the Amanjaku switched the tags around so I could afford these boots that were a really good deal at even twelve dollars.

"Hey, I really do love your new outfit." Chloë's comment brought me back to school. "Did you buy that when you went shopping with me?"

"Wha . . . what?" I stammered. I could have sworn this was the real Chloë with me right now. I would bet my life on it! But then how could she have known about my shopping trip with the Amanjaku?

"Your mom bumped into us yesterday while we were buying groceries," Chloë answered my question without me having to ask.

"Oh, really?" I gulped. "What exactly did she say?" I suddenly started to sweat, so I undid the top two snaps on my jacket.

"She said, 'It was so nice of Chloë-chan to go shopping with Melony on Sunday,'" my friend told me. "The thing is, I had *no idea* what she was talking about." Then she shot an accusing glance my way.

I suppose this was the point at which I should have apologized. But instead I blurted out, "What did you say then?"

"I did what any friend would do," Chloë sighed. "I covered for you, of course."

"You did?" I wiped away the bead of sweat that had started to roll down the side of my forehead. "Omigod, *thank you*."

"I don't mind helping you out, Melony, but you should really let me know ahead of time. 'Cause then my mom asked *me* when I went shopping with you, and I had to lie that I went for a bike ride while she and Dad took our friends from California to a fancy restaurant. And then I got in trouble for not asking permission beforehand when they had asked me to stay home so I could take Kiko on a walk and clean my room."

"I'm really sorry," I finally apologized. Paying a few dollars less to the store than I should have didn't hurt anyone. Even so, I never meant to get the real Chloë in trouble. "Did they take away your phone?" In middle school, I'd found out that this was how a lot of parents punished my classmates. Even though I didn't have a cool phone, having it taken away sounded like it would be awful.

"What? No!" Chloë laughed. "I didn't get in *that* much trouble. After all, I actually was at home and had done my chores. So basically I just had to promise to remember to ask them first beforehand."

That's Chloë's definition of "in trouble"? If I had been caught in the same situation, my parents wouldn't have let me watch any TV and forced me to do extra chores for at least a week. I was relieved for my friend, sure, but . . .

Just then, Miasma and Scat came into view, walking toward us. I felt Chloë stiffen next to me as she wrapped her jacket tightly around her.

But instead of making fun of us like they did at random times before, they lowered their heads and veered several steps to the right to make room for us. Ever since they'd come back from their in-school suspension for drawing butts on the music stands in band class, they'd been different.

For instance, they no longer asked classmates if they knew how to "spell 'ICUP'" or signed up for teams or group projects as "Ligma Budd." Mr. Sutton had them seated apart in his class too. So, now they were as quiet as the Dread Pirate R. In fact, Scat spent most of class just watching the bunny hop back and forth in his cage. Sometimes, I even caught him feeding him a strand of hay that had fallen on the floor.

Not that anyone minded their change in behavior. At all! Although . . . I had felt a little twinge of *something* one day in science class during Miasma and Scat's in-school suspension, when we went outside and conducted experiments that involved mixing things together and causing reactions. We didn't blow anything up or light stuff on fire, but still, it was exactly the type of class Miasma and Scat would have liked. But they didn't get to participate.

Seeing their improved behavior since then made me realize that maybe our little Sharpie stunt was for their own good. They hadn't bothered me or Chloë once since then.

"You still haven't told me what you were up to." Chloë's scolding voice cut through my thoughts.

I told Chloë about my shopping trip with my mom and the lace shirt I was practically guilted into buying. "So I guess I just wanted to shop without her for once, and I knew they'd let me go if I were with you."

"I get it," Chloë replied. "Still, I don't like lying to my parents," she added with a grumble.

If you have parents who understand you, then of course you don't need to lie. A prickle of annoyance nagged and buzzed around me like a pesky gnat. Chloë said she "got it," but clearly, she didn't. How could she? *Her* parents didn't hover

over her every move, and act like dangers lurked in every corner of their dark, old house. *Her* dad didn't come home exhausted every night from working in a potato chip factory. Instead, Mr. Yoshida worked from home all day and probably relaxed with the ukulele when he needed a break. *Her* mom had a nice-paying job as a dentist, so having twenty-four dollars of spending money might not have been a big deal to my friend. Plus, Chloë had a big sister, so she probably never felt lonely like I did.

"Well?" Chloë prodded.

"I said I was sorry!" I snapped.

When my friend's eyes widened in surprise, I immediately wished I could take it back.

But the bell rang, signaling recess was over.

So I didn't.

Chapter FOURTEEN

"Y ou know what? Her parents had a new notebook shipped to her—from France!" I told Chloë as she sat cross-legged across from me on my bed. We were weaving friend-ship bracelets—well, at least *I* was weaving one. Chloë had stopped to listen to me with complete attention.

"I bet that cost a *fortune*." Chloë nodded.

"I mean, what Miasma and Scat did to her old notebook was really obnoxious, but there are a *lot* of notebooks that are probably way cheaper and just as good here, right?"

"Ugh, Chloë's *so* spoiled," Chloë responded. Only it wasn't really Chloë, it was the Amanjaku posing as her.

I was supposed to hang out with the real Chloë after school today, but she said "something came up." Maybe because I had been short with her and she just didn't want to come over, or because she really was busy. Either way, I was by myself. Again. I wasn't *completely* alone since my mom was downstairs working on her new quilt, but you know what I mean. There were some things I could talk to Mom about, but lately it seemed like we disagreed with each other on more things than we ever had before. The chores I could handle. I had been able to keep my grades up too. But despite how much I practiced, Miasma was still better at the piccolo than I was. And only the best players were going to be selected for the special ensemble, which meant my parents wouldn't let me go on the band trip. Even though I was trying my best, Mom just couldn't (or wouldn't) even try to meet me halfway.

I talked back to my mom the other day when she reminded me to clear my dishes *as I was clearing them*—or just *about* to, anyway. When I said, "I know, Mom!" she said that kids who sassed their parents like that in Japan would get in big trouble.

"But maybe this is because you're surrounded by all these American kids at school," Mom sighed. "Why can't you be nice and polite to me like Chloë?"

"Mom, Chloë *is* American." I was pretty proud of how calmly I was able to say this. Because I *wanted* to retort, *Geez, Mom, I hang out with Chloë more than any other kid, so maybe she's the bad influence.*

But I didn't because then I knew I'd get in trouble. And because what my mom said was true. Chloë *was* nice and polite. Way more than me. Which is probably why I felt like gossiping about my best friend more these days, and the

Amanjaku was more than willing to lend an ear.

But the second that the Amanjaku said Chloë was spoiled, it felt strange hearing my friend described that way. Being spoiled meant starting good and healthy, like a crispy apple, but then going rotten and mushy—bad. Like that girl Ashleigh who wore the most expensive clothes in our grade—we knew this because she told everyone what everything cost—and whose mom drove her to school in a Porsche every day. *That's* who came to mind when I thought of "spoiled." Ashleigh was tolerable in elementary school, but in middle school she'd become much more irritating. I didn't know what Chloë was like when she was younger, but she was far from rotten now.

"Remember when Chloë first arrived?" mused the Amanjaku-Chloë. She had untangled her fingers from the loops of embroidery thread we were using to make our bracelets. "Her mom let her sleep in and come to school later on her first day."

"Yeah?" I didn't see how that was spoiled.

"And then she had the nerve to *complain* about it."

I didn't remember it that way. Chloë was nervous about being the new kid, and sleeping in had meant she'd be new in her morning classes the next day too. Sure, I was a little annoyed when she complained about having to lie to her parents for me. But it wasn't *her* fault. It wasn't mine, either. I truly did believe that the real Chloë had come to the door that day. So, if we were really looking at who was to blame, it was sitting in my room with me right now.

To be honest, I was getting tired of the Amanjaku. Earlier this afternoon, I was bored and wished I could hang out with someone when it just appeared in my bedroom. After my initial surprise, I didn't mind having it there because at least I knew who it really was. And by bypassing the front door, we avoided the situation we ran into when the real Chloë had to cover for my shopping trip with the Amanjaku. Seeing how it could disappear into the school bathroom or when biking around corners, I knew that even if Mom barged in, the Amanjaku could just vanish if necessary.

But now I kind of wanted it to go.

Next to me, the Chloë-wannabe stiffened and her hands gripped the quilt covering my bed, almost like she was hanging on. She suddenly looked pale, almost like she was . . . fading?

I finished my bracelet and got up to search my desk for a pair of scissors. I needed them to cut the extra strands so they wouldn't bother me when I wore it. They were underneath my report on owls, whichI still had to revise and turn in as a final draft to Mr. Sutton. *I'll ask it to leave*, I thought. *I have better things to do with my time.*

"She *is* spoiled," the Amanjaku insisted. "Did you hear about her phone?"

I stopped rummaging around my desk for a second. I hadn't, but I wasn't sure if I should let on that I cared.

But I did.

New Chloë loosened her grip on my bed and pulled out

a phone from her back pocket. "She lost her phone. And you know what her parents did?" Her cheeks flushed pink as she whispered excitedly. "She wasn't even punished at all. They bought her a new one. Just like that!" The Amanjaku snapped its fingers.

Lost? Or stolen?

"I know what you're thinking." New Chloë raised an eyebrow at me. "What does it matter? She has a new phone. And now—"

New Chloë handed her phone—the one with the sparkly flower design, the one that I'd envied ever since our very first time hanging out—over to me.

"It's yours," she said.

When she placed it in the palm of my trembling hand, I thought it might be the one the Amanjaku had left for me after our first afternoon together. The one that disappeared when I looked for it later.

But it wasn't it. It was definitely Real Chloë's phone. When the Amanjaku first said Chloë had lost her phone, I suspected that it likely had a hand in it. But having my suspicions was entirely different from having them actually confirmed.

Even though I should have given it back like a hot potato, and even though I knew it was the wrong thing to do, my hands moved like they were possessed, and they snatched the phone from the Amanjaku.

I couldn't do anything with it, though, because I didn't have the passcode.

Suddenly, New Chloë took the phone, looked at it, and then handed it back to me.

It was unlocked.

"You should go to 'settings' and reset your passcode," Chloë instructed. "You can't use my face to unlock it when I'm gone."

I did as the Amanjaku suggested.

This is wrong, I thought. *For one, would the Yoshidas still be paying for it? Whose plan was it on? Could they track it using Find My Device?*

"Details, details," New Chloë mused. "You don't need to worry about that," she assured me, her voice cool.

Although I did wonder for a fleeting moment how it could access doubts I hadn't voiced, the Amanjaku interrupted my thoughts with an enthusiastic "There are some great piccolo tutorials online."

That's right! This phone could benefit us all. I would use it to help improve my piccolo playing. My parents would be pleased.

"Okay," I answered without feeling the need to question her any further.

If this magical being who could appear and disappear at will said it was fine, then who was I to argue? I was mesmerized at everything I could access. Recipes, cooking videos, classmates' social media accounts showing all these aspects of their lives I hadn't known about. The best slice of pizza ever. A close-up of a ladybug on someone's nose. A really fancy cupcake with a whopping dollop of frosting drizzled with raspberry sauce.

I would check on those piccolo tutorials later.

As I played with my friend's old phone, I felt New Chloë watching me. Studying me. But when I looked up, she was back to weaving the rest of her friendship bracelet.

"Is it long enough?" She held it up to my wrist and tied the ends in a knot. "Fits perfectly!"

At that moment, I heard footsteps approach down the hall. I shoved Chloë's phone under a pile of papers on my desk.

Chloë sat up. She jumped off the bed and into my dark closet. With a wink, she pulled on the closet light's string. She giggled and then disappeared right as it sparked on.

A quick knock on the door and then my mom was standing in my room before I could even tell her to come in.

Typical Mom move.

"It's dinnertime," she announced as she scanned my room. It was clean, for once, so she couldn't say anything about *that*. "Who were you talking to?"

Oh, so that's *why she's acting all suspicious*, I thought.

"Chloë," I answered without missing a beat. I pointed at my cheap phone with all the parental controls on it. It was charging on my nightstand. Even I was surprised at how easily the deception came to me now.

I held my breath, though, as I hoped my mom wouldn't check my call log. Turns out that my mom trusted me more than maybe I deserved.

My mom looked relieved. "She's such a nice girl," she said. Again.

"Yeah, she really is," I responded with a smile.

"Just be quick, all right? Dad's home early. We can eat all together tonight." With that, my mom shut the door.

I took Chloë's old phone out and typed in my new passcode. It unlocked.

Such a nice girl, I said to myself. *Or is she?*

I tucked my new phone into the back of my desk's top drawer.

Later that evening, after I had said, "Oyasumi nasai" to my parents, showered, and tucked in for the night, I pulled Chloë's—I mean *my*—new phone out. I tapped in my passcode and it opened.

Finally! Finally I had a new phone, that window to the world I had wished for. But instead of checking out all that the digital universe had to offer, for some reason, I tapped on "photos."

Those were all still Chloë's. The real Chloë's.

But I scrolled through them anyway.

What I noticed first was just how many photos she took of her dog, Kiko. Holy moly! Extreme close-ups, him smiling, him frowning. On his back for tummy rubs, stretched out on the grass in a flying-Superman pose, sleeping. Him in midstride as he ran toward her and another really cute one of her hugging him (and him looking like he was just barely tolerating it).

Then there were the ones of her family. Emily with her palm outstretched to the camera in a "don't you dare take a photo of me!" pose. Chloë's mom and dad dressed up to go out. A short video clip of her dad playing the ukulele and singing a jaunty Hawaiian tune.

And then there were photos of us. Some of these I remember posing for. Like the selfies at my house during that first time she came over. But there were others I hadn't realized she'd taken. Like one where I was devouring a slice of pizza at her place. I didn't look happy, though, because that was after my parents had denied me the chance to sleep over. And another one of me at school reading a book on the steps by the track. Probably waiting for her so we could walk around together.

"Ugh, Chloë. Stalker much?" I said to myself. I smiled, though, when I saw that she had favorited that one.

There was another one of Chloë standing in front of the Rosecreek Middle School sign. Even though she was smiling, it couldn't hide the fact that she was also nervous and scared about attending a new school.

Then there were photos that her mom must have taken. Image after image of Chloë holding up different outfits with a big sincere grin on her face. I recognized a lot of them. They must have gone shopping for new clothes before moving here.

I scrolled farther down. Pictures flashed before my eyes as I looked through what kinds of things mattered to my friend.

Crimson-red autumn leaves highlighted against a clear blue sky. Sunshiny-yellow dahlias with blooms that filled the screen. A green caterpillar with spots. A video of a butterfly flapping its wings. A clip of Chloë playing a tune on the piano with a bird whistling in response at the window. Emily must've taken that one.

But then I came to the end. The last photo was of the cover to her fancy (expensive!) notebook from France. There were no images of California or what her life was like before she moved here. She *had* mentioned that she was given her mom's old phone, so maybe that was just before she came to Oregon.

In any case, my friend was—without question—a beautiful soul. With a beautiful life in which it was clear she had everything a girl could possibly want.

I powered off the phone, feeling *very* conflicted.

Finally, I had a phone.

But it belonged to my friend.

She lost it, though. And her parents bought her a new one without even punishing her for being so careless!

She won't miss it, said a voice inside me that I hardly recognized.

But it's wrong, another voice answered.

I'm tired, I told both of them before I closed my eyes and willed myself to sleep.

Chapter FIFTEEN

The following week at school, another one of my wishes came true.

The time had come for the special ensemble auditions. Since Ms. Delgado didn't want to take up class time, everyone who wanted to try out had to schedule a slot after school over the following week.

The deadline for registration commitments was approaching. While other students would have to wait until everyone had played to find out whether they'd made the special ensemble, Ms. Delgado made it clear she would choose only one piccolo—and both Miasma and I wanted that spot. The thing about him, though, was that *he* didn't need to make the ensemble to be allowed on the trip.

But I did.

Whether my parents would grant permission for me to go would depend on my performance today.

"Come on in." Ms. Delgado invited me into the band room where only Miasma sat. Before the Amanjaku and I had gotten him and his friend Scat in trouble, he'd always be completely turned around in his chair, making faces, or up to some sort of nonsense like launching pencils straight up into the ceiling to see if they'd stick.

After, though, he became much more serious. And he actually became even *better* at the piccolo. He looked pale now, and he rested his instrument on one knee as the other bopped up and down nervously.

The music for the special ensemble was *way* harder than what the rest of the band played every day. Using my new phone to access tutorials, I practiced more than I ever had over the past week. But would it be enough to beat Miasma? I sure hoped so.

I sat down in the open chair next to my nemesis but scooted it a foot away. I expected Miasma to make some sort of snide comment, but he didn't. In fact, he was beginning to look downright ill.

"All right, Melony." Ms. Delgado sat at her desk near the front of her room as she shuffled a couple sheets of paper around. "Shall we start with you?"

I nodded and took a deep breath. *Please*, I thought.

I raised the small silver piccolo to my lips and began. The first note was strong and true. I counted the rests correctly and didn't rush. At the tricky rhythm section, the one where I had to play a triplet followed by a scale of eight sixteenth notes, I made sure I was even and steady—*tri-pl-et, one-e-and-ah, two-e-and-ah.* I might not have played the audition material as quickly as it should have been played, but I was consistent and only hit one wrong note.

"Very nice, Melony." Ms. Delgado scribbled a few notes down. "Are you ready, Hunter?"

Miasma cleared his throat a couple times before he began.

Screech! His first note was a little too strong, and sharp as well.

Bewildered, he brought down the piccolo. "Uh, do you mind if I start again?"

Ms. Delgado nodded. "Sure, go ahead."

The second time, the same thing happened. As he was about to ask for another chance, Ms. Delgado encouraged him to keep on going. "We all make mistakes. It's how you work through them that matters. Just do your best, okay?"

Miasma continued, but he was so rattled by his shaky start that his slipups snowballed, one after another. It was hard not to cringe by the time it was over. Ms. Delgado, to her credit, acted like Miasma's last note wasn't making her ears water with how out of tune it was.

"Bit of nerves, huh, Hunter?" she asked, her eyes sympathetic.

"Yeah, I just didn't sleep well last night." Miasma mumbled.

"Totally understandable before an audition." Ms. Delgado nodded.

"It's not that," he mumbled. "Something was tapping on

my window all night. As soon as I was about to fall asleep, it started again. Do you think I could have another—"

"Now, Hunter." Ms. Delgado didn't allow him to finish. "I've given you a second chance, after the Sharpie incident, you know."

Hunter nodded, miserable.

Ms. Delgado turned to me. "Well, Melony. I must say, you've improved so much! I'm quite impressed. We will need to pick up the tempo a little bit for the actual performance, but I'm very confident you'll be able to handle it. We'll have additional practices once the rest of the ensemble is selected. How does that sound?"

I gulped. I could hardly believe it. "That sounds great, Ms. Delgado," I answered.

"Hunter." Ms. Delgado turned to a very despondent Miasma. "Thank you for trying out. But you understand why this part goes to Melony, right?"

Hunter grunted. "Yep." He didn't look at either of us as he packed his piccolo in its case and left the room as quickly as he could.

When he did, I could swear I heard a giggle and footsteps padding softly down the hallway in the opposite direction.

But when I peered out, I saw nothing.

I earned this, I told myself. *I did!* But for some reason, vanquishing my enemy didn't feel quite as good as I imagined it would.

When my dad came to pick me up, though, I could hardly

contain my joy. "Otousan, I did it! I made the special ensemble!" I shouted as I slid into the back seat. I couldn't quite see his entire expression, but in the rearview mirror his eyes crinkled as he responded, "Yokatta ne, Melony-chan! Very good!"

Later that night, my parents officially registered me for the school band trip.

"I knew you could do it, Melony-chan," my mom said softly.

Truth is, *I* didn't know I could do it. But I did. I did everything they asked, and I had earned my spot. This trip, this bit of freedom! And all through my own efforts, with no help from that silly Amanjaku.

But then, a thought shoved itself into my mind like someone else was willing it there. *You might have had some help.*

I didn't ask you to keep Miasma up all night! I thought back.

What about the tutorials you accessed using that phone you always wanted? The voice inside my head was insistent.

The happiness I had been feeling dimmed.

Chapter SIXTEEN

The following week, we had a rare afternoon of sunshine. So, Chloë and I took our lunches outside and sat in the grassy area in the center of the oval track. It was warm enough that we didn't even need our jackets, so we spread them out to sit on.

I took two bags of potato chips out from my lunch sack and held them up to Chloë.

"Which flavors today?" she asked. Any awkwardness that had hung between us since I snapped at her about my lie had finally all disappeared.

"I have nori wasabi, which is kind of spicy, and lemon basil."

"Oooh, they both sound good." Chloë looked back and forth between them. "I'll try that one."

I handed her the nori wasabi bag.

She ripped it open and pulled out a chip. "Hey, look!" She

held it up to me. "I'm surprised your dad let this one slip by."

It was a chip shaped like . . .

I giggled. Chloë followed suit.

"A butt!" I burst into full-on laughter that made me snort juice out of my nose. I tried to hold it in—after all, I'm sure Chloë was still a little sensitive about all the butts Miasma and Scat had drawn in her notebook. But she was guffawing now too.

"I'm cursed." She coughed as she wiped tears of laughter from her eyes. "I can't get away from them. I gotta show this one to Emily."

Then she pulled out her new phone, all the humor seeming to drain from the moment. I felt ill, remembering that I had her old one stashed in my desk at home.

"Is that a new phone?" I asked, even though I knew the answer.

"Yeah," Chloë responded as she took a photo of the unfortunately shaped potato chip. "I have no idea where the other one might have gone. I've looked everywhere! Checked the front office lost and found, too." She frowned. "I would have asked you, but I figured you'd let me know if you had seen it."

I nodded. *It's not lying if you don't say anything, right?* Honestly, it was getting hard for me to tell anymore. "I'm sorry. You probably lost all your photos, huh?"

"Nah, I had just backed those up the night before." Chloë shrugged as she returned her phone to her pocket. "I never had a new one, always hand-me-downs, like the last one from my mom. I guess that's why my parents didn't make a big deal about buying me this one."

Spoiled. Just like the Amanjaku said.

I began to feel less and less guilty about having Chloë's old phone. She didn't even seem to care it was gone!

I let out a sigh of relief. How silly it had been of me to worry so much about what was wrong and right. It's not like anyone was getting hurt.

"Before I forget"—Chloë popped the butt chip in her mouth and wiped the flavor dust on her shirt—"I have something for you!"

She pulled out a notebook. It was beautiful, with autumn trees on the cover and bits of gold sprinkled among the leaves—and very similar to the fancy French one that had been defaced.

"For me?" I gulped. ". . . Why?"

Why would she give this to me when it was *her* notebook that was ruined?

"Why not?" Chloë giggled. "Plenty of good pages left in my old one. Plus, look!"

Chloë shoved a couple more nori wasabi chips in her mouth as she retrieved her own notebook from the small backpack she carried her lunch in. She flipped through the pages, and while some had been torn out, for the rest of them, she'd done something quite amazing.

Where Miasma and Scat had drawn butts, she changed

them into a bouncing basketball, a beaded necklace, a cater-pillar, a butterfly.

"Get it?" Chloë asked. "A BUTT-erfly." And then she slapped her knee as she laughed, clearly delighted with her truly awful, un-funny pun.

She stopped, though, and made a face. "Whoa, these chips really are . . ."

"Spicy? I told you—"

"Oooooh . . . aaaahh!" Chloë waved a hand in front of her mouth.

I handed Chloë her water bottle and she chugged. When she had finished, she shook her head as if to clear it.

"Tell your dad this flavor's the *best*." She gave me a thumbs-up. "I loved them!"

I smiled. "That'll make him happy." I opened my new notebook. Signed on the front page was a note:

To Melony: The best friend I could ever hope for.

You know that saying "When life gives you lemons, make lemonade"? Well, life didn't give Chloë Yoshida lemons. It gave her a bunch of butts, and instead she made butterflies.

It gave her me as a friend, and what have I done?

Chloë wasn't spoiled. She was a sweet person. A truly good friend.

And the Amanjaku was bad.

I closed my new notebook, knowing what I needed to do.

Chapter SEVENTEEN

asked Chloë if she could come hang out late tomorrow afternoon. She agreed with a cheerful "Ooh, yes! Then I can tell your dad how much I loved the new potato chip flavor!"

A few days ago, I might have thought that she was sucking up. Now I knew that she was genuine. She just really liked nori wasabi potato chips.

How could I have doubted her?

My heart felt like an anchor in my chest. I had to give back her phone and explain everything. I thought about fashioning some sort of tale that made more sense, but I was done with that. I was done with the lying and the half-truths. That's not who I was.

Chloë came to my house an hour early, but she said it was because her mom and dad didn't want her to be at their place alone. Unlike my parents, who calculated the risk of a weird babysitter as higher than letting me be by myself, the Yoshidas always insisted that Emily watch over Chloë when they couldn't be there.

"Is it okay if I come over now?" Chloë called before coming over.

My mom was supposed to be home by the time Chloë had originally said she'd be here. She had run out, though, to grab some groceries. My dad was here, but he was napping. But I didn't wake him up to ask because he was snoring and was so tired he even slept through the phone ringing. So, I figured he must need the rest.

When Chloë arrived, she explained, in a strangely vague way, "Turns out Emily had . . . a thing she needed to be at."

I didn't think too much about it, though, because *I just wanted to get this over with*. I also held on to a sliver of hope that Chloë would be okay with what I had done. That she would not only believe in things like the Amanjaku, but that she would accept that it made me do these things. That she would forgive me.

She had biked over, and just like she did the first time she visited, she brought snacks. But they were the artificial neon Fruit Roll-Ups I loved instead of the healthy clementines that had initially impressed my parents.

"It's okay, right?" she whispered conspiratorially, as she eyed my dad, still sleeping on the sofa in the living room.

As soon as she spoke, my dad shivered and muttered in his sleep. "Jun, doushita no? Jun, abunai yo . . ."

"Yeah, those are great," I assured her. I just wished I was hungry enough to enjoy those sticky, chewy treats.

My dad seemed to quiet down when he heard my voice.

"What was he saying?" Chloë asked.

"Nothing," I responded as I hurried down the hall toward my bedroom and motioned for Chloë to follow. "I think he was just dreaming about an old friend of his."

In my room, Chloë spotted the notebook she had given me open and facedown on my desk. "Oh, cool!" she exclaimed. "What are you using it for?"

Truth is, I tried to draw something like Chloë did, but it wasn't very good. "Nothing," I mumbled. "Just practicing my . . . signature."

I don't know why I lied to her like that, and I prayed she wouldn't ask to see.

She nodded. "Well, show me when you feel ready," she said in the most understanding way. "Or not. It's your notebook now!"

I exhaled. She really was the nicest person ever.

Then we did our usual things. Used her phone to make silly videos. Gossiped about who got in trouble at school. But Chloë knew something was up. Of course she did—she was my best friend.

"I . . . I have something to tell you," I started. I went to my desk and rummaged through the top drawer. I found her old phone and handed it back to her.

And then I confessed *everything*.

Once I finished, Chloë was really quiet—so silent that I could barely stand it. Anything would have been better than her stillness, this absence of words. Screaming, yelling, even an accusatory "How could you, Melony? I thought we were friends!" would have been better.

But there wasn't any of that. Finally, she said in a low, quiet voice, "So, do you promise not to see this Amano . . . Aman—"

"Amanjaku," I finished for her. "I know, it's so unbelievable, but I swear I won't ever see it again. It's bad, I know, it's just that there were times when I was feeling trapped and—"

"I get it." Chloë looked up and nodded at me slowly. "I know what it feels like to be trapped. I do."

My heart leapt, like it was being freed from the anchor that had been weighing it down all day. I had hoped beyond hope that Chloë would be understanding, but I was also prepared for her to not want to be friends anymore.

She stood up and stared out my window. "Hey, are those persimmons?"

With that, a wave of relief washed over me. Was Chloë really ready to move on from this, just like that?

"Uh, yeah," I answered, wondering if that meant I was forgiven. "Do you like them?"

"Had them all the time in California." Chloë continued to stare. "They look ripe."

"The guy who lives there is real mean," I said. "I've always wished we could pick some, but—"

"Do you?" Chloë interrupted me. She turned around and met my eyes when she asked, "Do you *really* want them?"

A thought flashed into my mind that the way she asked was kind of weird and intense, but then Chloë immediately followed up with, "Because I know Mr. Chase. He's actually really nice."

"You do?" I asked. Chloë had never mentioned this before.

"Yeah! We met him when we were out walking Kiko one day. He said to come over anytime and to pick what we wanted!"

Leave it to Chloë and her super-nice family to get to know our neighbors before we did. I couldn't wait to tell my mom ("See? There was nothing to be afraid of").

Chloë grabbed her jacket and ran down the hall. I followed a few steps behind. I couldn't believe it! She wasn't upset. I still had my friend.

By the time I found a small container for the fruit and made it out the back door, Chloë was already halfway up the tree.

"What are you doing?" I yelled up at Chloë. "Let's just pick the ones that are lower!"

"They're not as ripe!" Chloë hollered down at me.

"Be careful!" I yelled. My mom would never forgive me if I let Chloë get hurt on my watch. She reminded me of a monkey with how quickly and easily she made her way through the branches. I never realized that Chloë was quite this daring. Unless . . .

I let out a sigh of relief when she started making her way down. But then she held out her hand. "Come on! There are a couple *perfect* ones up there!"

"Uh . . ." I looked around. I'd wanted to do this for years—every autumn when the persimmons ripened, I'd wished I could climb up and enjoy them before the birds got to them.

"You should tie your shoe first, though." Chloë pointed to my unraveled laces, just like she did when we first became friends. *How silly I'm being,* I thought as I tucked the plastic container under my arm and bent down to tie my shoe. But as soon as I stood back up, Chloë grasped my hand and hoisted me onto the first branch. She yanked with so much force that I dropped the Tupperware I'd brought outside.

"There you go." Chloë made sure I had a good hold of the branch. "Now follow me!"

I did as I was told, and finally, we reached two unblemished, plump, deep orange persimmons near the top of the tree. There was a nice, sturdy branch there, too, so I clung to it. I wasn't afraid of heights, or at least I never thought I was, but we were up higher than I'd ever climbed any tree before.

I felt dizzy, but it wasn't just because I had looked down. It was with relief. *If this is how Chloë reacted to my confession, should I finally tell my parents about the Amanjaku, too?* I asked myself. *Maybe they would also forgive me as easily.*

I thought about bringing my persimmons back to share with my parents. I would present the fruit to them to sweeten their moods before I told them. Or maybe I would give them right afterward as a peace offering.

But the container remained on the ground, and I didn't have any pockets to carry them.

"Let's just eat them up here," Chloë suggested. "If we dropped them, it would be such a waste."

What Chloë said made a lot of sense.

Persimmon skins are a little tough, but once you get past the peel, the fruit is soft and ripe. I sighed as I bit into one. "Omigosh." It was every bit as delicious as I imagined it would be. Persimmons could be bitter to the point of making your mouth pucker, but not this one.

The sun was beginning to set, turning the sky orange and the clouds the color of lilacs. The spectacle was almost as magnificent as the sensation of the sweet persimmon in my mouth—firm and tender all at the same time.

Chloë had already finished hers. She scanned the other branches for more as she waited for me to finish.

"So, does this mean . . . we're good?" I asked my friend as I wiped the sticky orange juice from my chin. This afternoon, so far, had gone so much better than I had imagined it would.

"Actually," Chloë replied. She looked down. "I *am* a little hurt."

My heart fell like the persimmon skin I had just dropped. *I knew it.* I *knew* she had been way more understanding than any friend—even a best friend—could be.

"How can I make it better between us, Chloë?" I asked.

More than anything, I wished I never took her phone, or ever hurt her.

"Who, who, who?" Bob, the barred owl that so often frequented our yard, fluffed his feathers in a tree nearby. I had never seen him so close before. There was an urgency in his eyes I never expected to see in a bird. In fact, his expression was almost . . . human?

"I've given you everything you've wished for, right? What has your friend done for you that I haven't?"

My last bite of fruit slithered down my throat and hit my stomach like a brick.

This is not the real Chloë.

"I have wants and wishes too," the Amanjaku sighed sadly.

Voice, check. Eyes, check. Even her smile today was a spot on—a dead ringer for my best friend. *How could I not have known?*

Ever since the Amanjaku appeared in my life, it had gotten harder and harder to tell right from wrong. Seems like it also affected my ability to figure out who was my friend and who wasn't.

"I only came to you when you wished for me." The Amanjaku sounded sad as it twirled the stem of a dead brown leaf between its fingers. "You wanted someone to play with, so I showed up. You wanted the freedom to buy your own clothes, so I made that happen. You wanted your own phone, so I got you one. You wanted to go on that trip to California, and thanks to me, you have your parents' permission. Did you ever think what *I* might have wanted?"

I gulped. Truth is, I hadn't.

"Of course you didn't. All you think about is what *you* don't have. You never think about anyone else."

"That's not true!" I retorted, even though I knew it was. A little bit.

My thoughts spun trying to think of all the times I *had* thought about others, and . . . I couldn't think of anything. But I never do well under pressure—and this was *a lot* to deal with right now!

"Your friend Chloë, though. She always thinks of others. But it's easy to when you have everything. And your friend really does have quite a lot, doesn't she? Especially compared to you. It's so unfair!"

I thought about all the times I compared my situation with Chloë's. Her easygoing parents with my more anxious ones. Her home filled with music and laughter and my quiet one with my mom's weaving song often the only sound to break our gloomy silence.

"Do you want it, Melony? Do you *want* to be her? To have her life?" The Amanjaku dropped the leaf it was twirling and grabbed on to my hand.

"What? No!" I wrenched myself free from the Amanjaku's grip. I mean, I *might* have at some point, but not *seriously*. Not to the point that I would ever, *ever* do anything about it. What did it mean, anyway, "to have her life"? Alarm bells went off in my head at the very thought.

Although it still *looked* like Chloë, I wondered how I ever could have been fooled. This was no New Chloë. This was False Chloë, Evil Chloë, a farthest-thing-from-Chloë-Yoshida-that-you-could-get.

"You girls," the Amanjaku hissed. "You have everything, but you don't even realize it. You still want, want, want. Well, if *you* don't want to be Chloë, then maybe *I* will be."

I gasped—I couldn't believe what I was hearing. The Amanjaku said it came when I wished for it, now I concentrated as hard as I could into wishing it to be gone from my life forever.

Fake Chloë had begun to clamber down. "It's not that easy!" She paused several feet below the top branches where we had sat. She seethed. "Every time you wished for me, you made me stronger. Every wish you accepted from me made it easier for me to become part of this world. *Your* world. Now I'm here to stay!"

I would NOT let this evil *thing* take the place of my friend. I shimmied down after it and grabbed its arm.

"Go AWAY!" I yelled at it. It struggled to escape my grasp as I held on to it with one hand and to a tree branch with my other. A gust of wind made the tree sway, and I almost lost my balance for a second. We were both still so high up that the ground seemed to spin below us, but then I found my grip—and my determination—again. "I want my *friend,* not you. I don't want you around anymore! So, stop acting like Chloë—I'll never be fooled by you again!"

The Amanjaku paused for a moment. "You don't wish me to be Chloë anymore?"

"No, not ever!" I yelled. "Go AWAY!"

It stared at me, and I glared back, refusing to give in. And then, as our eyes locked, something amazing—amazingly *terrifying*—began to happen.

"Very well, then," it answered.

My hand, where it grasped the Amanjaku, began to tingle. I tried to let go, but my fingers wouldn't release their hold. Jolts like electricity spread up my arm.

Fake Chloë's straight hair began to curl and frizz, her cheeks plumped out and reddened a bit . . . like mine.

Like *me*. The Amanjaku no longer looked like Chloë, but now, as I gazed upon it in horror, I felt I was looking into a mirror.

"It took so much effort to be her anyway. I couldn't manage it for more than a few hours at a time before I was completely exhausted. You, on the other hand . . ." The Amanjaku no longer sounded like Chloë. In fact, its voice reminded me of my own.

"You and I, we're not so different. Wouldn't you agree?" the Amanjaku asked.

I felt myself nodding before I realized what I was doing. "No!" I shouted. I shook my head back and forth like I was trying to jar its comments loose from my brain. "I am *not* like you! I am—"

But before I could finish, New Melony snarled at me.

"You got your wish, and now I get mine." In one horrible movement, the new me grabbed on to my other arm.

Her nails dug into my skin, and she yanked with such force that I fell—

Down . . .

Down . . .

Down.

The wind whooshed past my ears. I reached out and tried to catch hold of something, *anything*, as I tumbled past branches that scraped and caught on my feathers.

My . . . *what?*

I stretched out my arms, but in their place were wings— cream colored and striped with grayish-brown bars.

As the ground rapidly approached my face, I tried to scream, but all that came out was a loud "Who, who, who, whoooo. Who, who, who, whoooooo?!"

The classic call of a barred owl.

I flapped in a desperate attempt to save myself from a certain death.

Once, twice . . .

The leaves on the ground rustled as I whooshed past them. I flapped again and propelled myself into the dimming late-autumn sky.

Chapter EIGHTEEN

Flap, flap, soar.

Any minute now, I'll wake up, right?

Flap, flap, soar.

This has *to be a dream.*

I thrashed around, but instead of finding myself in my bed, I spiraled and looped in the sky until I felt woozy.

Flap, flap, soar.

Any way you looked at it, I was an owl. And by all accounts, a *barred owl*.

Right after "the change," I narrowly missed flying myself into a tree by my house. I avoided an epic faceplant by grabbing on to a branch with my foot, which actually ended up being talons, and by using my arm-wings to hoist myself upright. I took a few moments to gather my breath, to try to make sense of whatever it was that had just happened.

But then, I spotted another barred owl—the one I called Bob—fly right at me like a torpedo.

That's when I flew as far away as I could. If the Amanjaku could change me into this, and it disguised itself as Chloë and then me, there's no telling what else it could do. I'd always been happy to see Bob, but not then.

After who knows how long and who knows how far, my wings began to feel heavy, and I knew I had to stop and rest. I had never seen a bird free-fall from the sky from exhaustion, but if it were ever to happen, I imagined it would happen to me.

I looked around and didn't see Bob, or anyone or anything else that could have been the Amanjaku, so I swooped down, down, and stretched my talons out to land in a wide, open meadow. I thought I had decreased my speed, but clearly not enough since I landed with so much force that I skidded and then tumbled—beak over feathers—for several yards before I came to a complete stop. I turned my head to scan my surroundings. First to the right . . . and then when I was about to turn and scan to my left, something inside my head whispered, *You don't have to.*

That's right! Owls could turn their heads almost all the way around.

I gave it a shot, and just like I learned in the research I did for my report, I was able to confirm that I could swivel my head about three-quarters of the way before I had to turn it back. If I weren't so weirded out about the Amanjaku stealing my identity and turning me into a bird, I would have thought it was cool.

Where am I?

In my hurry to escape, I hadn't paid any attention to where I was flying. I just knew I had to get away. Up high, where I'd found myself soaring, I rode the gusty breezes for a while before I decided to land. But now I was lost.

Could owls be lost?

I never learned about that in my research.

I rested in a patch of dried grass and wondered what to do next. I lived near a river—I mean, *Melony* lived near a river.

Then, a pair of glowing eyes appeared through the brush. I blinked and they disappeared, but I knew I didn't imagine them. All my senses went on high alert as I froze in place.

Sure enough, within a minute, the yellow eyes appeared again, only they were closer this time. I was bone-tired, but I forced my wings to move. And not a moment too soon!

Sharp teeth gnashed at me as I willed myself to flap as hard as I could.

Once I was up in the air, I looked down at a gray coyote snarling and shaking a feather it had pulled from my tail.

Flap, flap, climb. Flap, flap, soar.

The sky was a deep black, darker than I'd ever seen it with only pinpoints of starlight poking through the clouds. The glow from the streetlamps and the lights shining from cars and houses barely reached where I was flying.

I wasn't attached to anything right now, not even the ground. I guess this is what it felt like to be free. But all I could think of was getting back to where I was from.

The inky ribbon of river wound along the ground like a snake. Remembering that I was gliding with the wind to when I landed in the meadow, I flapped against it this time. The cold night air pushed against me, and chilly gusts hit my face like needles as I propelled myself as fast as I could toward where I thought home might be.

Although I had felt completely drained only minutes before, as the night deepened, my strength returned. I felt sharper, more determined. Owls are mostly nocturnal, I realized. I had forgotten this from what I'd read in class, but I felt it in my blood as it pumped through me and gave me the energy I lacked before.

I followed the river until suddenly I saw a huge reddish oval underneath me.

The track!

It had to be the one at Rosecreek Middle School that Chloë and I had trudged around. How many times? For some reason at this moment, I wished I had kept count.

It took my parents less than ten minutes to drive me to school. My home *had* to be nearby. I circled down, closer, closer.

A large green space. The park? Trees. Roofs.

And then, the brilliant crimson of our Momiji—the Japanese maple in our backyard—shone through. *Bloodred*, my mom had said. On this darkest and most alarming of nights, those words described it perfectly.

Something scurrying in the woods diverted my attention, though, and before I could stop myself, I dove toward it. Without even realizing that I was doing it, I grasped on to a squiggling, squeaking mouse.

The Melony part of me was horrified at what I had done, but the owl part of me was also—all of a sudden—*starving*. I gulped it down headfirst. I couldn't tell if it was the mouse still squirming and twitching in my stomach or my disgust at what I'd just eaten that was making it flip and flop. I knew I had to try to keep my meal down, though, to gather some strength.

"Oyasumi nasai." I heard Melony's voice—*my* voice—through the woods as she said good night to my parents. It carried through the dense thicket, through the walls of the house that I now flew toward. My wings flapped and crashed through the tree limbs that got in my way.

There she was, in my room, wearing my pajamas, looking very much like me—Melony Yoshimura.

"*Mom! Dad! Be careful! The Amanjaku is back!*" I shouted from outside the back door.

But "Whoo, whoo! Whoo whoo, whoo!" was all that came out.

Even though their blinds were drawn, I flew at my parents' bedroom window with all my might and *thumped* against it. Even though it hurt, I did it again. And again. *Where are they? They* have *to notice the racket I'm making outside.* But they didn't. Had they already gotten ready for bed? Or maybe my mom was still at the dining room table engrossed in her quilt? Or had the Amanjaku already done *something* to them? Again and again, I flew, scratched, and tapped at the glass until I had to stop and rest for a moment from exhaustion and pain.

A light turned on in the kitchen, so I mustered what remained of my energy and half hopped, half flew toward the window.

But as luck would have it, the Amanjaku was there, not either of my parents. Its eyes locked with mine. Then it smiled.

Get out, you imposter, I hooted.

The new Melony stared at me coolly. *Are you enjoying your freedom?* she communicated back, but without speaking a word.

My birthday felt like a forever ago. *You know that's not what I meant!* I jumped up and down on a branch. The remaining leaves shook and quivered like my rage. *I'm going to get back at you, I swear.*

Instead of being scared, New Melony put her hand in front of her mouth to hold in her laughter. *Oh, you are, are you?* Her thoughts invaded mine.

Then she rummaged through a drawer and found a box

of matches. She brought them to the window as if to show me what she found. Then she lit a match and held it over the kitchen sink—just like I did before the Amanjaku arrived. Then her expression grew distant and wistful, like she was wondering what *she* should wish for.

I concentrated on my own wish with all my might:

I'm gonna make you pay for all the trouble you've caused, mark my words—

But then she did something that took my breath away, that chilled me so much that I felt like I was going to choke on the shriek that caught in my throat.

She brought the flame closer . . . and closer to the lace curtains that framed our kitchen window. *I don't think so,* her hardened eyes told me. *Because I think you'd regret what I'd do.*

I shook my head, but still, the match was so near the curtains, I was sure that they would ignite in a blaze any second now. The flame was almost at her fingertips but she showed no sign that the heat was hurting her—at all. Instead, a small, cruel smile danced around her lips.

"Melony, nani shiteru no?" A question from beyond the kitchen. "What are you doing?" If I had tear ducts, I would have cried at the sound of my mom's voice.

I think you'd better go. New Melony's thoughts ran through my head like the roar of a train.

Although it was the hardest thing I'd ever had to do, I tore myself away from my home. If I didn't, the Amanjaku would make sure that there would never be one for me to return to, ever. Before I reached the sky, I turned around and hovered just long enough to make sure New Melony blew out the match that threatened to burn down my house and the two people I loved most in the whole world.

Chapter NINETEEN

New Melony is more like Evil Melony.

She does what she wants and only thinks about herself.

I know this because I was her, and even though I'm not her anymore, I watch the new me over the next few days and I know what she is.

I have found a little hiding place in the Douglas fir right outside Mr. Sutton's classroom. The glare from the morning sun would make it hard to see inside its windows. But because afternoon clouds blanket the sky today, I can observe what she does as me from behind the branches thick with evergreen needles, at least while she is in that class.

At school, she turns in my report, which I never had time to revise. Or maybe I did, but I might have gotten distracted by things that don't matter to me now. In any case, she doesn't put in the work needed to finish it, though, because she simply doesn't want to.

She doesn't care that Mr. Sutton looks disappointed when he hands my paper back to her. Why would she? I did the work, and she is not me, even though no one notices yet. The last few pages of my report, the part that I hadn't had a chance to perfect, are covered in blue ink. There is no grade on it, only a note that says, *See me after class for revision opportunity.* I don't think she will, though, since she rolls her eyes and then crumples it up when the teacher is not looking.

She does care, however, about the special fountain pen that did the correcting.

"Class, has anyone seen my pen?" Mr. Sutton asks the next day when he opens its fancy case and finds it empty.

Everyone looks around, including Chloë. Evil Melony looks so innocent, but I know she did it. I know she took Mr. Sutton's favorite pen. I know because when I was her, *I* had thought about what it would be like to use it. I never took it, though, because I knew it was wrong. Evil Melony doesn't seem to know, though.

Or she knows, but just doesn't care.

The next day, Mr. Sutton isn't there and the class has a substitute.

We are working in groups today. I mean, *they* are working in groups today. When I was Melony, I didn't like group projects, but the teachers all said it was good for learning how to cooperate with other people. *You mean, how to have one person do everything while their classmates take the credit without having done their fair share?* is what I used to think. Still, I did the work. I always did the work.

Not Evil Melony, though. She's retrieved Mr. Sutton's fancy fountain pen from her backpack and is writing nonsense on the poster. And misspellings galore! When we did group posters in the past, I wrote in pencil because I liked to consult with my group members before committing to our answers in pen or marker. They hardly ever disagreed with me, but I still went through the process even when I didn't want to.

But Evil Melony isn't like me. Instead, she's making mistakes on purpose. And peering inside the window from where I'm perched, I can see why.

She's in a group with Miasma and Scat, and no big surprise there, but they haven't done anything. I bet they thought Melony would do it all for them. They look a bit nervous, like they can tell something is a little different about the quality of this poster compared with ones *I* did before. Evil Melony just smiles and tells them, "Don't worry. I got this."

My owl heart squeezes tight again when I think about why she's being an awful group member—so she can bring those two boys down with her. I admit, sometimes I *had* thought about what it would be like to sink my group and our shared grade by doing absolutely nothing. But I never actually followed through with it! Because I cared.

Chloë's eyes grow as big as my owl ones when she catches sight of Evil Melony with Mr. Sutton's missing fountain pen.

She opens her mouth to say something, but then the substitute stops her.

"Focus on your own work!" she scolds, when both Chloë and I know that the real me is the last person who would ever goof off with Miasma and Scat during class.

At recess, Chloë paces back and forth in front of the steps by the track. She has her notebook in one hand and taps the palm of her other hand with it. Only, it's less like a tap and more like a slap, over and over again, like she's mad at it. But I know it's Evil Melony she's angry with because she never shows up. Instead, she is with the arctic circle kids. They take selfies together. Evil Melony wears my boots that cost twelve dollars, but that I only paid $8.40 for. She wears a jacket that I don't recognize. It's puffy and long and it looks just like the jackets all the other "cool" girls wear. I have no idea where Evil Melony could have gotten it or when.

How has Evil Melony made her way into this posse of middle schoolers who have deemed themselves popular? First, she acts unimpressed with them, which seems to make them work harder to impress *her*. Overall, her attitude toward them is scornful, which I admit, is a little bit how I felt toward them when *I* was Melony. But it was only because they didn't like me. Or maybe I wanted them to notice me and they never did.

Occasionally, this Melony will throw an approving look the girls' way. But not too often, or her status will drop in their eyes. It's a little social dance, with "blink and you'll miss it" cues that I never participated in.

From the steps near the track, Chloë watches as her best friend ignores her completely. Her brows knit together and she looks more concerned than mad now.

"Whoo, whoo!" I try to catch her attention. But she's too focused on Evil Melony to notice the owl in the Douglas fir just a few wingspans away from her.

Once the children leave and the sun sets, my empty stomach and my need to survive take over. As much as it grossed me out before, I catch and gulp down small snakes, rodents, even large bugs that I catch with a *crunch!* of my beak and gulp with a *squish* down my throat. Tonight, I do all my hunting at once until my stomach is full to bursting. My mother would have told me to stop, but she's not here to give me that sort of advice. I hope that this extra food might let me sleep now so I can stay awake more during the day.

On my second morning as an owl, I open my eyes with the sun. It feels strange to do so since normally this is when owls wind down and get ready to rest. At least that is what feels more and more natural to me.

Evil Melony is up even before my parents are (or are they her parents now?). How strange! When I was me, I liked to sleep in. Surely my parents will notice the difference?

But they don't because their new daughter tiptoes as quietly as a cloud down the hall to the foyer where my dad hangs his keys on a hook and sets his wallet on a ledge. She unfolds the brown leather—faded and worn smooth from years of use—and takes out three bills. She places it back exactly where it was before and slinks back down the hall like a shadow. She hides the money inside the notebook Chloë gave me, and then tucks that in the very back of my bottom desk drawer. She climbs back into bed.

From a place where Evil Melony cannot spot me, I watch her from her bedroom window for an hour before my alarm goes off. It blares for five minutes and still Evil Melony doesn't move. *Why isn't she waking up?* I wonder. But then I remember how I used to sleep through my alarm as well.

"Melony, okinasai!" my dad's voice echoes down the hall.

"Melony, hayaku!" My mom bursts into my room and pulls off my covers.

Their new daughter lies still for a moment before she stretches and groans—*exactly like I would have. I* am almost convinced she is Melony Yoshimura.

"Okay, okay," Melony grumbles. "Geez, chill," she mumbles to herself.

Is that what I sound like? I am embarrassed for Past Melony.

Then, I watch as Melony assembles her outfit for the day. It's the three-dollar shirt from the Red, White, and Blue my mom suggested I buy and a pair of sturdy, no-nonsense jeans. I coo a sigh of relief until I see her slide my closet open and pull out an outfit that had been hidden in the back. I can't see what it looks like, only that there are tags that she bites off with her sharp teeth. She rolls the clothes tightly and stuffs them in the bottom of her backpack—to change into in the school bathroom whenever she has the chance, no doubt. How do I know? Because I've thought of doing this before.

For breakfast, Melony opens a bag of my dad's artisanal potato chips and eats them.

"Melony!" my mom says with a frown. "Potato chips are *not* for breakfast."

"They're not?" the Amanjaku-disguised-as-me asks innocently. "But this new flavor . . . miso, is it? It's *so* good! And we have miso soup for breakfast sometimes."

I cannot believe how manipulative the Amanjaku is. And how good she is at it, too!

"You're right, we do." My dad contemplates what Evil Melony has just said.

Since when do I eat chips at all? I try to remind my parents. *I eat cereal for breakfast. Or do you not remember me?* My last hoot trails off like a sad *coo.*

"Stop!" my dad commands.

I perk up. My dad knows something is up!

Evil Melony pauses, her chip halfway between the bag and her mouth.

"I can't believe I let that one get by me." My dad points at the chip in the Amanjaku's hand. He chuckles to himself. "What do you think? What does that look like to you?"

From outside, I bob and turn my head to get a better look. I gasp. It looks just like a rabbit—in fact, with its slightly burnt section, it is exactly like the Dread Pirate R!

Melony examines the chip. She turns it upside down and

around. *How can she not see it?* Finally, she shrugs. "I dunno. It doesn't look like anything to me." And with that, she pops the chip into her mouth and crunches.

My dad looks more disappointed than surprised. "I guess you're getting too old for these games, huh?" he says more to himself than Melony.

"Yeah, guess so!" she scoffs at my dad. He looks sad and shuffles away without another word.

No! I flap my wings. *I might have acted like I was getting too old for these games, but that one was so obviously a bunny. I could see it. You know anyone who was your real daughter could see it, right?*

I want to be back in my body. I don't want this owl one. Sure, I don't have to spend hours in a classroom or be confined to the school grounds, but I don't care. I want it all back.

What can I do? All I know is I can't do this alone. After all, I am only an owl.

Chapter TWENTY

"Who?"
Who am I?
I am Owl.

At night, I fly and I listen. I swoop, catch, then *gulp!* I eat. It is a simple life. I am free.

Even though I go wherever I want, whenever I want, I am drawn to two places the most. During the day, I rest in a large tree close to where many fledgling human creatures flit about and play. They are called "children," I think. It is noisy here, but if I can stay awake, I like to peer into the box where they sit for long periods of time.

There is a white-haired big human and he talks more than the children. Golden circles frame his eyes so that he actually reminds me of a wise old owl. There are two girl children who intrigue me the most. They both have black hair and brown eyes, but that is where the similarities end. One is nice. I think if I were a girl, we could be friends. The other reminds me of someone I once knew. She wears sturdy beige things around her feet with white fluff that peeks out of them like the wool that covers sheep. There's something about the way she scans the class—like she's hunting for prey—that makes me not like her at all. At night, I survey the dark for my food so that I can survive. In that way this girl and I are the same. Still, there's something about her that makes my feathers ruffle.

Today there is tension inside the box. Why? Who knows.

The white-haired man asks, "Melony? Can you collect everyone's homework, please?"

Melony, the girl I don't like, sighs long and loud. She doesn't answer him or get up.

"Is there a problem?" There's an edge in the man's voice that says, "You better get up now, or there will be consequences." He doesn't say that, but I can hear it. Owls have very good hearing.

The Melony girl gets up and papers *rustle, rustle,* as students pass them to each other and then to the girl who puts zero effort into her collecting task. She stands in one place with her hand held out. The papers make their way to her, but it is taking a long time, even by owl standards.

"Hey, Mr. Sutton?" After handing his paper to Melony, a boy stands by the cage that houses a plump, splotchy rabbit.

The white-haired man's foot bounces up and down while he sits at his desk "Yes, Jay?" He calls on the boy, but his eye is on the paper-collecting girl. He sounds impatient.

"Does the Dread Pirate R ever get any exercise? I mean, if I were in this cage, I think I'd like to get out some time."

"I take him home with me on weekends," the man answers. "I let him hop around my kitchen then."

"You do?" Jay looks like he didn't expect to hear this.

"Of course," the man says. "Some evenings too. I promise I do."

Jay does not look like he believes the man. Why not? I don't know.

"I wish I could get you out," the boy mumbles to the rabbit. To my owl ears, what he said sounds like a shout to me, but no one else seems to have heard. Except for maybe Melony, whose eyes glitter at his wish.

"Excuse me," the nice girl speaks up as she taps the other girl on the arm.

The one called Melony pauses. "What?" She answers in a way that sounds like a threat. The nice girl doesn't seem to notice, though.

"I forgot to write my name on my paper," the nice girl responds in a voice like a song sparrow. "Would you mind writing it for me? It's the one on top."

The mean girl looks like she wants to hack up an owl pellet onto the nice girl's head, but the white-haired man says, "Go ahead, Melony."

Melony glares, grabs a pen, and scribbles:

CHLOE

She shows the paper to the nice girl. "Happy now?" she asks with a sneer.

The girl's eyes widen. "You forgot the umlaut," she says in a voice barely above a whisper. Then, more loudly, "You forgot the umlaut."

"The what?" Melony asks.

"Ne . . . Never mind," the girl responds. She looks toward the man to see if he heard. It seems like he did because he looks concerned now too.

How could this Melony girl not know what an umlaut is? Even I do, and I am just an owl.

"Who, who, who, whoooo?" a voice beside me asks. It is dark now and the hunting has not been good tonight. The last thing I need is another owl to compete with.

Even so, I respond, "Who, who, who, whooooo" on instinct.

To my surprise, another barred owl—like me!—is on a branch across from mine. It bobs its head up, down, and around.

"*Pata pata pat-tan,*" it says next.

I have never heard barred owls hoot this way before.

However, in a breath, I respond, "*Tat-ton ton.*"

"Finally! Finally, I have found you!" the owl screeches with excitement. "It was not easy. There are a *lot* of barred owls in this area, you know!"

I did not because I made sure to avoid them. I'm not sure

why, but spending my time alone—without attachments—just seems safer.

"I asked them all, but none knew how to respond. In fact, several even attacked me. I'm sure they thought I had been affected by some brain-eating amoeba!"

"I'm sorry, do I know you?" I ask this owl who seems to recognize me, but I'm not sure we've met ever met.

"Don't you remember?" it asks. "I am the one you called 'Bob' in the past."

Bob? I search my owl brain for a memory. *Bob the Barred Owl* pops up into my mind. Images of it in my backyard, or was that the mean girl's backyard? Following me on a bike ride with . . . was that the nice girl with the umlaut in her name?

"Bob?" I turn to him, confused. It is my impression I've never seen him before, yet I also *do* feel like I know him somehow.

"Yes, that is what you called me!" He hoots and flaps his wings. "Even though that is not really my name."

"Oh?" I ask. "What is it, then?"

"Jun," he replies. "I was once a boy called Jun."

"Oh." I feel like that should mean something to me. But I don't know what.

"And you were once a girl called whoo—" The owl stops, blinks, and re-collects itself. "Whoo, whoo, ooo . . . riko. Uriko? Have I finally found you, Uriko?"

For a moment, I feel dizzy, like someone has just picked

up my world and tilted it sideways. Suddenly, this story pops into my head as images flash through like lightning.

> *Once upon a time*
> *(A dinner table, birthday cake, presents)*
> *In a small Japanese village*
> *(A girl blowing out candles)*
> *There was an old man and an old woman*
> *(Her parents . . . my parents?)*
> *Who wanted a child more than anything else in the world.*
> *(A potato chip in a box, set next to the one that looks*
> *like—)*

"Jun? Like the boy in the potato chip?" I exclaim to Bob. "Are *you* that friend?"

"Yes. Yes! I am so happy that you are you!" The owl bobs and dances again. He lifts a feathered foot and chews on it like he can't contain his glee.

"The Amanjaku took over my body too," Bob continues. "I'm sorry that it has targeted you now. But there's hope! Your family and friends—I think they will believe!"

I wish I knew what Bob—I mean Jun—is talking about.

"You! They will believe *you* are their daughter. Not that imposter in there! *You* are their Uriko, their Melony, their Uriko Melony Yoshimura!" With each name he hoots, Jun pokes at me with his beak.

I am . . . *who?*

I am . . . ?

I am!

This knowledge hit me like a clap of thunder. I wobbled and wavered on the branch, like all my owlness was leaving my body at once. Then, all the memories of my life as a girl came flooding back. Not only ones of my birthday and my wish, but my friendship with Chloë, how I first met the Amanjaku, the Sharpies, the shopping trip, the phone, the ensemble audition. Everything about the Amanjaku and how I had gradually let it invade my life.

Jun spread out a wing and steadied me as I sidestepped down the branch. When I reached the trunk, I leaned against it for support.

"But . . . how? How can I get back?" I asked. "How can I get back to where I'm supposed to be? To *who* I'm supposed to be?"

"They are on the brink of realizing it." Jun said as he preened. "You must make them recognize you. Let them know how sorry you are for all the trouble your wishes have caused. Make amends!"

"Make amends?" I asked. "I'm stuck in this owl body. What can I possibly do?"

Jun looked at me kindly, his black eyes encouraging. "There's *always* something you can do," he hooted gently. "Even as an owl."

"*I'm* not even sure who Melony is anymore. I had lost sight of myself long before I became an owl," I cooed sadly. "What if I can't? What if Evil Melony really is no different than the Melony I used to be?"

Jun's expression darkened. "But you must. You must get back into your body as quickly as you can," he warned me. "The Amanjaku wants and wants, and soon it will realize your body is not enough to obtain all it desires. It will use it to the point of destruction and then move on to another."

"Is that what happened to you?" I asked. "How were *you* tricked by the Amanjaku?"

Jun sighed. "My parents were strict. Very strict."

I nodded. "I sure know how that is."

"Hoo, hoo, hoo, hoo," Jun laughed. "That's what you think *your* parents are? Please. Hoo, hoo, hoo! Don't be ridiculous."

For a brief moment I thought about flying away, because I didn't like how Jun was making fun of me. "Oh yeah? What did your parents do to you?" My curiosity made me stay.

"It was a different time back then. We cut our hair according to school guidelines and wore uniforms to our classes. But we didn't complain much. It was all we knew! But my parents made me study every free moment I had. Even after school, I went to another school to study some more. Sunday was a day most people relaxed, but not me."

My parents did nag me about whether I'd done my homework. Or practiced my piccolo. But they never made me go to school after school. Sure, I had a lot of chores, but I did have free time too.

"More than anything I wanted some time for myself. To do what *I* wanted to do."

This was beginning to sound familiar. "And that's when the Amanjaku arrived?"

"In the form of a new classmate who became instantly popular. He was charming and effortlessly smart. And fun! So much fun. Everyone wanted to be his friend, but he acted like he enjoyed my company the most. Sometimes we would just hang out at the local convenience store to buy a snack before my parents noticed. It was no big deal. After all, who were we hurting?"

A memory of my first afternoon with the Amanjaku flashed through my mind. The extra cookies. The mess we made. But we cleaned it up. No harm, no foul.

"But then, we started to sneak out more. Instead of buying snacks at the store, he'd take some without paying for them. I would, too. Just for the thrill."

Like my shopping trip to the Red, White, and Blue. *Did switching the tags really hurt anyone?* I had thought at the time.

"Your father noticed, though. When he tried to explain that stealing from the store hurt the store owners, I laughed at him and said they probably didn't even notice. When he told me the store clerk got fired, he made me feel bad. I tried to tell him it wasn't me, that it was the Amanjaku, the demon spirit who feeds off people's darkest desires. That people who've met the Amanjaku want to do things that might not be allowed otherwise. Go places that they shouldn't."

"Did he believe you?" I asked, even though I already knew the answer.

"Of course not. He got mad at me for thinking he'd believe such an outlandish tale. I became angry with him for not standing by me when I needed him most. That's when we stopped being friends."

"Oh," I sighed. This explained why my father looked so sad when he first told me about Jun. "If it's any help, I do think he believes you now."

"Well, that's too little, too late, don't you think?" Jun snapped his beak at me. "When it came time for our big entrance exam—the once-a-year test my parents had asked me to study so hard for—I didn't show up."

"What happened to you?" I asked, wanting to know the answer and dreading it at the same time.

"People said I probably ran away." Jun paused to tuck his head under a wing for a moment, like he was trying to hide from the truth. He mumbled, "My parents never stopped looking until the day they . . ."

It was clear Jun didn't want to revisit this part of his past. I'm not sure I really wanted to know all the grisly details either.

"How come *you* didn't forget who you were?" I pressed on with my questions anyway.

"I did." Jun swiveled his head away from me. "That is, until my human body was no longer."

Until his human body was no longer? Alarm bells went off in my head. Was that what the Amanjaku was planning for *my* body? And did that mean Jun was . . . dead? But he couldn't be; he was right here!

"Is that when you became an owl?" I was barely able to get the question out, but I had to know the whole story.

"No." Jun emerged from his wing-tuck and fluffed his feathers. "I became a raven first."

"Then why are you an owl now?"

"The life span of a raven is only ten to fifteen years."

"Ohhh." I nodded in understanding. "So when your raven body died, how'd you become an owl?"

"If you must know, I followed your family here. To watch over all of you." Jun sidled away from me on the branch we shared.

"You did?" I hooted in surprise as I scooted back toward him. "That was nice of you."

"But the journey over the ocean exhausted me. I felt my body giving way once I arrived, but then I met this owl. He was mean—attacked runners when they went for their evening jogs. One time we got in a tussle over a snake we both wanted and . . ." Jun's voice trailed off.

"So you took over his body?" My eyes widened as I remembered how the Amanjaku grabbed on to my arm and became me.

"Remember, he was a jerk! I did what I had to do." Jun clacked his beak defensively at me.

Even though I was grateful for Jun's presence, it surprised me that he had to do the same thing to the owl that the Amanjaku had done to me.

"It will be the last time," Jun answered like he knew what I was thinking, his expression tormented like the one in Dad's potato chip.

Then he swooped off the branch in pursuit of a mouse so I couldn't ask him anything more.

Later, Jun and I hatched a plan. Who had my wishes hurt? So many people. I wanted to make things right with my parents first, but Jun pointed out how close the Amanjaku was to them. If it knew we were working together now, who knows how it would react.

"I cannot make people recognize you, or mend what you have broken." Jun fluffed his feathers. "Only you can do that. But I can watch over the Amanjaku and alert you if it decides to do anything drastic." I nodded in agreement.

"You must remain vigilant," Jun added in loud hoots. "It is easier than you think to lose sight of who you are."

"I know." I answered with more attitude than I meant to. *Boy, do I know*, I thought.

Seemingly satisfied that I understood, Jun flapped his wings and left me alone once more.

Chloë. Maybe I could try reaching her first. My best friend knew something was up—I could tell by the way she looked at Evil Melony when she refused to put the umlaut in her name. That I would never choose the arctic circle over her. Chloë also knew me well enough to realize I would never *steal* something from Mr. Sutton. But didn't I take her phone? No, the Amanjaku was the one who did. I *tried* to return it, I swear!

I zoomed toward her house. In addition to wanting to make things right, I ached for the warmth I knew I'd feel at the happy ukulele melodies I hadn't heard for what felt like so long.

Sure enough, there was music playing at her house, but it wasn't from any instrument. The Yoshidas had their record player on, and the songs echoed throughout an empty room—filled only with sadness and tension. This was a far cry from what I had been expecting.

On a telephone pole outside their house, a sign was posted. It was a picture of Kiko, foxlike and smiling. It read:

LOST SHIBA INU
REDDISH-ORANGE WITH A WHITE CHEST AND PAWS.
MISSING SINCE 11/25
PLEASE CALL 503-555-0102 WITH ANY INFORMATION

Kiko missing? Why? Why would anyone want to run away from this happy home? I thought to myself.

Mr. Yoshida was in the front yard, walking back toward his house. He carried two signs in his left hand.

I swooped down and landed right in front of my friend's father.

"Whoa!" he exclaimed. Then he stopped and looked around to see if anyone else had witnessed my strange behavior. There was no one.

I hooted and strutted—actions very unusual for an owl. I hoped he knew this.

He took out his phone and began recording. "What brings you here, Mr. Owl?" he asked me.

I was so excited he hadn't shooed me away that I wasn't even bothered he called me "Mr."

I stopped and swiveled my head 270 degrees to the right, and then 270 degrees back around to the left for him.

This made his eyes smile. It was the first time I noticed they were tired, like my dad's. But I didn't think my actions made him realize that it was me—Melony—his daughter's best friend trapped in an owl's body. That would be a lot to expect from anyone.

"What are you doing?" Mrs. Yoshida's irritated voice cut sharply through the dusk.

Mr. Yoshida looked guilty and pointed at me. "Look at this, honey! I think he's doing some sort of mating dance."

Ugh! Gross, Mr. Yoshida! I stopped and thought for a moment. I didn't know what else I could do to let them know it was me. I spread my wings as wide as they would go.

"Oh my goodness, it looks like it's going to attack you."

Mrs. Yoshida opened the door wide for Mr. Yoshida. "Come inside quick so it doesn't bite you and give you rabies."

Mr. Yoshida seemed almost sorry as he made his way to the front door. "Bye, buddy." He looked over his shoulder.

It's bad enough that my attempts to communicate hadn't worked. But now I was also slightly offended that Mrs. Yoshida thought I was rabid. Owls can't transmit rabies!

I flew closer to their kitchen window and listened in. Luckily, owls have very good hearing.

Mr. Yoshida tried to show his wife the video he took of me.

"I can't believe you were playing with your phone when Kiko is still missing, not to mention dinner not being ready." Chloë's mom dismissed him.

Mr. Yoshida put the phone in his back pocket and set a pan on the stove top with a *clatter*.

"For your information," he grumbled, "I was *not* 'playing on my phone.' I had just spent the last two hours canvassing the whole neighborhood, putting up signs—"

"Sorry, sorry." Mrs. Yoshida sighed and suddenly looked very tired. "I just wished we had gotten Kiko the GPS collar when I suggested it."

"Yes, and that was in the same sentence that you asked how my job search was going."

Job search? Chloë told me her dad worked from home. The way my friend's parents speak to each other now is so different from how they seemed when I came over before.

"That didn't mean I didn't want to get him the collar."

"You mentioned *three* times how expensive you thought it—"

Three stomps and a *slam!* interrupted their argument. Mrs. Yoshida rubbed her forehead. "What now?"

Mr. Yoshida strode down the hall to Chloë's room, where the noise had come from.

I silently flew toward her window and perched in the tree just outside it.

My friend was on her bed hunched over her phone. She was looking at something that was making her shoulders shake . . . with laughter?

No, with tears. She was sobbing. Whatever was bothering her was on that phone of hers, but still, she scrolled and scrolled.

"Chloë?" Her dad knocked on the door.

My friend didn't answer—she just cried harder.

Mr. Yoshida opened the door and rushed to Chloë's side when he saw how upset she was. Chloë's mom appeared in the doorway and hurried over to comfort her too.

"What's wrong, sweetie?"

"You can tell us, baby!"

"I'm never going to escape them." Chloë sniffed. "No matter where I go, they're always gonna find some way . . ." She grabbed her pillow and sobbed into it before she could finish her sentence. She dropped her phone on her comforter and her mother picked it up.

When she saw what was on her daughter's phone, her

face twisted from concern to anger. Even from where I was, I could see her cheeks redden like they were filled with lava from the inside. "Those little—"

Mr. Yoshida patted Chloë's back. "What do those girls matter? They're selfish and mean, and who cares what they say? You never have to see or talk to them again if you don't want to."

I was so confused. Chloë hadn't said much about what her life had been like in California, but she hadn't let on that it had been awful. Other than that time Miasma and Scat had drawn butts all over her book (which would upset *anyone*, I would think), very little seemed to bother her.

"I'm going to call their parents," Mrs. Yoshida grabbed her own mobile and began taking photos of Chloë's phone screen.

Even though I was amused by how Chloë's mom took screenshots, I was reeling from how different life was at Chloë's place than how I imagined it to be.

"What about Melony?" Mr. Yoshida was still trying to comfort my friend. "She's a good friend. Do you want to invite her over?"

At his question, Chloë stopped crying long enough to emerge from her pillow faceplant. "Melony is . . ."

I leaned in. *She's different. Say it, Chloë, please, I know you sense it.* I tried my hardest to send my thoughts to her. To will her into getting her dad to help me.

"She's, I don't know . . . not herself lately."

Yes! I knew it, I *knew* my best friend in the whole world would notice.

In my excitement, I flapped my wings and bobbed my head and hooted up a storm. So much so that Mrs. Yoshida stopped her yelling into her phone at someone who probably deserved it to peer out the window.

"It's that rabid owl again!" Mrs. Yoshida frowned. "Do you think I should call animal control?"

"No!" Chloë yelled. "I mean, what if someone called animal control on Kiko? You know how he gets when he's scared. Have you . . . did any of the neighbors say they'd seen him?"

My friend searched her dad's face with pleading eyes. When he replied, "No, but don't worry—we'll find him," they filled with tears again.

Chloë's mom started to close her curtains. *No!* I thought. Somehow, in some way, I needed them to notice me. I flew straight at the window with my outstretched talons.

SMACK! Mrs. Yoshida jumped back. I reeled backward from the impact—I hadn't meant to hit the window that hard. But Chloë looked my way. For a second, our eyes met, and I swear she recognized me.

That is, before I fell to the ground in a daze.

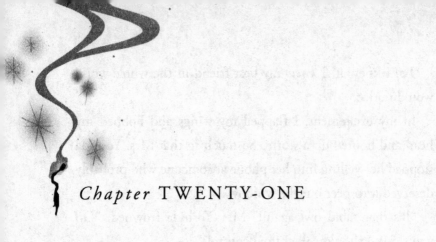

Chapter TWENTY-ONE

After the stunt I just pulled, I was 99 percent certain Mrs. Yoshida was going to call someone to catch me. And since she was pretty convinced I was rabid (I really wished she could read my report so she'd learn that owls don't get rabies!), I had a hunch it wasn't going to be some nice organization that would patiently try to translate my hoots into English.

Who? Who else have I wronged? As I soared away, I knew who I must visit next.

I flew toward a house I had always admired. It was on the river and its front yard was a lawn like thick green carpet. Cherry trees lined its driveway, and every spring their blossoms were like an explosion of pink confetti. I had never seen inside, though, since it was gated off. But now that I was an owl, I could fly over its roof and peer through the windows.

I loved this house, but I had never liked the person who

lived in it. That didn't matter now since I needed to make things right if I wanted to be myself again ever. I landed on the deck railing and peeked into a bedroom that reminded me of a bird's nest in its messiness. A boy sat in the middle of it all, with his back toward me.

Tri-pl-et, one-ee-and-ah, two-ee-and-ah, notes from a piccolo floated on the wind.

Unlike in the audition for the special ensemble, Miasma played it perfectly this time.

A man with slicked-back black hair streaked with gray talked to himself as he paced in the hallway outside of the room. He wore a neatly pressed white collared shirt and gray slacks. On his feet were black dress shoes that shone like they had just been polished. "Yeah, but we don't have the budget for that, so that puts us in a bit of a bind," he said to no one in particular. Then I realized he must be on a call.

Miasma continued to play—from memory and without his sheet music, I might add. *He's better than me,* I begrudgingly thought. Still, on the day of the audition, I beat him fair and square. My feathers ruffled.

"Would you mind if I called back in a couple minutes?" The man finished his call as he tried to close Miasma's door. A pile of dirty laundry kept him from being able to.

"Hey, buddy. I'm trying to do some work. Would you mind taking a break or playing downstairs?" the man asked.

Miasma stopped playing. "But, Dad, I have a chance to earn back my spot on the ensemble. Melony is really screwing up these days. It's like she doesn't care—"

Dad? I guess that made sense, but this businessman didn't seem like Miasma's father at all. For one, he was all put together and professional while Miasma was just a mess. But the man didn't seem like anyone's dad, in fact.

"Hunter." The man rubbed his eyes like he was very, *very* tired. "I get that you have a crush on this girl, but I don't know if taking her place in the ensemble is going to make her like you—"

My head spun from the information revealed in this discussion. Evil Melony was going to lose my spot? My hard-earned trip to California? But even worse than that . . .

"I do *not* have a crush on her!" Miasma objected and turned as red as a tomato at the same time.

"Who, who, who, whooooo!" I also exclaimed at his dad's ridiculous observation.

But his father continued like he didn't even hear either of us. He shoved Miasma's clothes away from the door with his foot. "Don't you think it's time to give this up, Hunter? Look, you promised you'd do baseball this spring if we let you try the piccolo."

Miasma looked like he was about to burst. And who could blame him?

"But I don't like baseball. I like—"

"This girl, I know, I know," Miasma's dad interrupted, even though it was clear he didn't know *anything*. "Just try to play a little quieter, okay?" And with that, the man gave one last tug on the door and slammed it shut.

At the same time, a gust of wind knocked me off my perch, but that wasn't the only force that had thrown me off balance. A *crush*? Ew! A crush meant that you secretly like someone. No way did Miasma have a crush on me—because you don't act like a jerk to someone you like. And if he really did like me and was just being annoying because he didn't know how else to be . . . still ew!

I flew away from those thoughts *and* the weird, out-of-nowhere feelings of pity I was beginning to have for Hunter—I mean, *Miasma*—for how his dad worked more than listened to his kid. For how his father had an idea of who his son should be, but that didn't match the vision Miasma had for himself

Was it possible that Miasma and I were more alike than different?

Ew, ew, ew!

My attempts to reach Chloë had failed. I was still reeling from what I learned at Miasma's house. Who else could I try?

I didn't want to because I was almost afraid of what I'd find out there. But I had wronged him too, and I needed to figure out some way to make things right. And who knows how much time I had left?

The next place I flew to was small and old, with blue-gray paint peeling on the outside. The steady rain that had begun to fall shrouded the woods in a quiet hum. But the noise from the house cut through that. A television blared, but even louder were the shouts and yelling.

I landed on the handle of an overturned, rusty wheelbarrow closest to the glow from the living room. Inside, there was a lady with short bobbed and graying hair that was held out of her face with a plain barrette.

"What am I gonna do with you? First you get suspended, and now this?" She shook a handful of papers at a boy sitting with his back to her and his earbuds in—Scat.

Even so, I could tell he heard her by the scowl on his face.

"So lazy!" she hollered. "What do you have to say for yourself? A D? Really?"

It was the grade for the group poster project that Evil Melony sabotaged.

Scat crossed his arms and hunched over even more than he was earlier.

But this woman would *not* be ignored. She whirled around and faced him. When he turned his head to avoid eye contact, she yanked out his earbuds.

"Ow!" Scat finally acknowledged this furious woman in front of him. "What the heck?"

"These are the grades you bring home, even after I warned you? Why do I even send you to school? Why do I even bother with such a lazy—"

"Mom, I told you, I'm not lazy, I just don't—"

"Just don't what?" his mom didn't let him finish. "You just don't study? Gee, ya think I didn't know that?"

"I just don't get school! Everything is so much harder than it used to be, Mom. *Everything!* I have a hard time—" Scat's surly attitude began to crumble.

"You have a hard time because you don't try," his mom snapped back. Then she threw her hands up in the air and the papers went flying. "You know what? Do whatever you want. I. Don't. Care."

Back when I was still a human, my mom and I fought, but not like this. I felt a little sick when Scat's mom stormed out of the room. There was a time when I thought I wanted my parents to say something like "Do whatever you want" to me, but not like how she said it. My mom would never say she didn't care about me. She cared *a lot*. In fact, it struck me just now that a mother could never care too much.

Scat looked lost, but then he got up and stomped toward the back door, near where I was. With a *slam!* he was outside. He ran to an old oak and climbed up to a rickety wooden platform nestled among its branches. He pulled a phone from his pocket and called someone.

"Hi, Dad. It's me." And that's when the tears started.

I only heard half the conversation. "Yeah, um. I just wanted to thank you again for paying for the band trip, and . . . can I come live with you? . . . Yeah, I know. I know. It's just that, I don't know. It's like I'm trapped. . . . I try my best . . . but . . ." Scat paused and wiped his eyes. He swallowed hard and started again. "So there's, um, this bunny and it only has room to hop twice before he has to turn around, and I don't know. I guess I feel like him sometimes. . . . No, I don't want you to buy me a bunny, I . . . Yeah, I know. Next week, you promise? . . . Of course I believe you."

Even though I was only an owl, I could hear that Scat didn't believe the person he was talking to at all. I thought back to when Mr. Sutton assured him that he let the Dread Pirate R hop about his kitchen for exercise. Now I understood why Scat looked at him with so much distrust. I guess that must happen when you're lied to a lot.

"Yeah, okay. Love you too. Bye." When Scat finished his call, I could tell he meant what he said here. I hoped the other person could hear it too.

I should mention that it was Scat who was crying, not me. Because owls don't have tear ducts and I couldn't cry even if I'd wanted to.

"Who, whoo," I called to Scat gently. I doubted whether I could make him recognize me at the moment or make amends in any way. But when I was a human, I'd always thought it was special to see an owl. Maybe he felt the same way. "Who, whoo," I called to him again as I swiveled my head in a way that might make him smile.

Not only did I not cheer him up, but he threw a rock at me instead. "Go away, you stupid owl," he cried. "Just leave me alone."

So I did.

Chapter TWENTY-TWO

That night I flew for hours, looping around in the sky. Since I couldn't cry, I called softly into the rain clouds instead. I imagined they were like the pillow Chloë sobbed into. I wonder if that made her feel any better. I hope it did.

But when my hoots evaporated into the breeze, I only felt more alone.

Why would they pay attention to me when there was so much other stuff going on in their lives? I thought. *So much other stuff I had no idea about. No idea, no idea . . .*

BAM! All of a sudden, something hit me like a cannonball. I tumbled and spun in the air and when I finally righted myself, there was Jun.

"What the heck was that for?" I asked. Even though I wasn't spinning anymore, the world still was. "Was that you? Why would you slam into me like that?"

Jun hovered. "To snap you out of whatever funk you were in. Come! Melony is up to something!"

Without another word Jun zoomed like a torpedo toward where I used to live. I followed closely behind.

When we arrived at my home, all seemed as it should be . . . except for my open bedroom window. Carefully, Jun and I landed on the sill and peeked inside.

Evil Melony was nowhere to be found.

"Her alarm went off *early*," Jun explained. "That's how I knew it was plotting its next move."

The sun had begun to peek over the horizon, gradually lighting up her dark room. Which was neater than I had ever kept it—the bed was made and there wasn't a speck of dust anywhere. Jun and I hopped around. Inspecting. Listening.

"What could this mean?" I asked. My body had begun to tingle, like pinpricks of ice all over.

"It means your time is running out," Jun hooted. "Alert your parents! *Make* them recognize you! I will find the Amanjaku and keep it from destroying you and moving on to another . . . at least for as long as I can. *Hurry!*"

And with that, Jun flew out the window and left me alone.

Make my parents recognize me? I couldn't speak, I had no arms to pantomime anything. But . . . could I write? It was worth a try. I kept paper and pens inside my desk. Maybe if I could reach those? With one talon on the chair and the other one grasping the handle to the desk drawer, I pulled.

It didn't budge.

I tried again, this time putting some wing-strength behind it by flapping as hard as I could.

CRASH! My efforts not only opened the drawer, but caused me to knock over the chair.

I reached inside my drawer for something to write with. The first thing I got ahold of was a Sharpie with its cap on tight. As I tried to pull it off with my beak, I heard rumbles and thumps from my parents' room.

"Melony, daijoubu? Are you okay?" my dad's voice called.

Finally, I was able to pry the cap off. Maneuvering the marker was tricky, and my growing panic wasn't helping. What should I write? Where should I write?

There was no paper. Only my desk. I cringed remembering the trouble I had caused earlier with Miasma and Scat, but it was my only option. As quickly as I could, I wrote *I AM MELONY.*

But it was much harder than I imagined it would be to write with talons, so it came out like this:

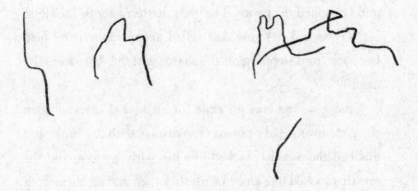

Darn it! There was no way my parents would get "I AM MELONY" from that. I was about to try again when I heard a gasp. I swiveled my head around, and standing in the doorway was my mother.

"Otousan!" she yelled for my father. "Come here NOW!" She rushed in, grabbed the pillow from my bed and threw it at me. I leapt into the air and flew down the hallway.

What else? What else could I do to make them know it's me? I flapped around the living room frantically.

"Where's Melony?" my dad asked as he emerged from their bedroom.

"I don't know!" my mom answered. "She wasn't here when I woke up, only this owl—"

Their footsteps came pounding into the living room. I grabbed a framed photo of me from the shelf next to the potato chip display and flew toward them.

Look, I pleaded with them. *It's me, it's me!*

But they weren't focused on what I was holding, only this owl in place of their daughter. My mom swung her fist at me, and I dropped the photo. The glass shattered across the floor.

"Ki wo tsukete!" my dad yelled at my mom as he held her back from stepping on the shards with her bare feet. "Be careful!"

That gave me enough time for an idea. I cracked open the glass to my dad's potato chip display with my beak, and grabbed the one that looked like Jun with my foot, and the one that looked like an owl with the other, and set them both on the living room sofa.

But that's not what my dad saw. "Kora!" he hollered. "It's eating my collection! Get out of here!"

I flew into the kitchen. *The tea!* I thought. *I served my mom tea.* She *had* to remember that, right? Crashing and flapping, I opened the cabinets. It wasn't like I had the time or ability to make her a cup now, but I could take out the tin of tea leaves, and—

"Stop!" Mom shrieked. She snapped a towel at me. When it made contact with my wing, I dropped the tin and the leaves spilled onto the floor.

All my efforts only seemed to enrage my parents further, but I couldn't stop—not until they realized it was me!

Next, I careened into the dining room, where my mom had been working on her quilt. On the wall, she had displayed her most recent prize-winner. The one with the Amanjaku on it, peeking out from behind a red Momiji.

I hated to do this, but they needed to know. I flew at the quilt, talons extended and landed on the Amanjaku. I ripped it from the quilt like I wanted to rip it from our lives.

I dropped the fabric square with the Amanjaku on it right in front of my mom, but she didn't notice. She threw the empty tea tin at my head, which knocked me dizzy for the moment. I wobbled as I tried to escape her fury—not only was my balance off, but my wing still stung from where the dishtowel had snapped.

My father, though, stood motionless in the living room.

He was staring at the two potato chips I had set out. "Jun?" he murmured to himself. He studied the one that looked like an owl and then looked at me, as if comparing us.

Finally. I could have wept from relief as I landed on the sofa, exhausted from the morning commotion. My mom rushed into the room but stopped when she saw my father. She was holding the piece of quilt. *Finally, they would connect the dots.*

My father looked straight into my eyes and I into his.

"Otousan . . . ?" My mother looked back and forth between the two of us.

". . . Amanjaku da," my dad whispered hoarsely. "What have you done with our Uriko?"

With that, he lunged at me and grabbed on to my tail feathers.

No! I hooted as my mom also rushed at me. "Amanjaku? What do you mean? This *owl*?!"

"Who, whoo! Who, whoo!" At that moment Jun appeared, flapping and beating his wings outside the living room window. "Melony, come quick! The Amanjaku—I found it!"

It was just the distraction I needed to escape my father's grip. I flew down the hall and out my bedroom window.

"Follow them!" my father yelled from down below. Their car started as I propelled myself after Jun.

Chapter TWENTY-THREE

"First, I saw her at the big house on the river," Jun explained breathlessly. "Then she left with a boy who climbed out the window."

House on the river? I thought to myself. That could only be . . . *Miasma?*

"I don't know what she said, or how she convinced him to go with her, but then they went this way." Jun veered into the woods beyond the main road that ran through town.

Ugh. Remembering the conversation between Miasma and his father, I had an idea of why he might go along with Melony and whatever evil scheme she had thought up. It still grossed me out, but I was pretty sure I was right.

"They ran along the highway for a while. The boy thought it was dangerous, but Melony just laughed at him. But the honks from the cars helped me keep track of them."

I followed Jun through a thicket of trees and ended up

on a rickety wooden platform nestled in an oak tree. From it, I spied footprints in the mud that led from the small old building— Scat's house—down a path leading away from it.

"Melony?" My mother's voice echoed faintly from where they'd stopped on the main road. "Otousan, did you see which way they went? Melony? Where are you?" Their footsteps crunched on leaves as they made their way into the forest.

"They came here next," Jun told me as he swiveled his head back and forth, scanning the surroundings for them. "But that's when I came and got you. Do you have any idea what they might be up to now?"

The morning sun illuminated their tracks. I hovered over and followed them through the woods toward a small creek. But that's where they stopped and no matter where I looked, there was no trace of where they could have gone.

Just then, a small brown bunny darted across the path and an overwhelming sense of hunger pushed all thoughts of Melony, Miasma, and Scat from my mind. My owl brain took over and I swooped down, talons outstretched, when . . .

I wish I could get you out.

Scat's words to the Dread Pirate R roared in my ears.

The way Evil Melony's eyes glittered at his wish flashed like lightning across my brain.

I swerved left and the bunny I had wanted to eat hopped underneath a rotting log, out of harm's way. I careened into a pile of soggy brown leaves and . . . Kiko?

"Grrrrrr . . . Yip!" A curly-tailed foxlike creature that was covered in dirt growled and barked at me.

I sat still and examined it more closely. "Kiko?" I hooted. "Is that you?"

Even though I knew he probably only heard, "Who, who, whoo?" he stopped and tilted his head at me, perplexed.

"What's the holdup?" Jun hooted down at me. "We have to find them!"

"The school!" I hooted back. "They're going to the school to free the rabbit."

Jun flew down and landed next to me. "Let's get going then!"

"I can't." I bobbed my head toward the pup. "I can't just leave Chloë's dog here."

Unless . . .

Jun swooped over my parents.

"There it is!" my father shouted. "Don't lose sight of it!" Out of the corner of my eye, I watched as my parents loaded into their car and raced after Jun.

I returned my attention to Kiko.

"What are you doing out here?" I asked him. "You've got your family worried sick, you know!"

Kiko whined in response.

"I bet you ran away for some fun but got yourself lost, didn't you?" I asked. To which he broke out into a doggy smile. *Yes! It was so much fun!* He then whimpered and howled sadly. *But now I totally regret it.*

"What if I told you I can lead you back to them?" I asked.

Kiko's ears perked.

I hopped from branch to branch. He took one step toward me, then another.

"And then can you help me?" I hooted.

Kiko answered with an enthusiastic "Yip!"

I flapped my wings and Kiko bounded after me.

Chapter TWENTY-FOUR

At school, the first students to arrive were huddled together, whispering.

"Who do you think did it?"

"Probably Hunter or Jay. They're always getting into trouble!"

"Yeah, but not the 'breaking into school' type of trouble!"

With each comment, my classmates' breath puffed out like smoke from a dragon. They burrowed their hands inside their puffy jackets and jumped up and down to keep warm.

Jun glided over and settled into the Douglas fir right outside Mr. Sutton's classroom. I joined him on the branch, but when I looked down, Kiko had not followed me.

Instead, he stayed hidden at the edge of the woods.

"Kiko, come on," I hooted.

Kiko whimpered and hunkered down, his tail uncurled. When I looked over, I saw why.

It was because *I* had arrived.

I mean, it was the Melony who looked exactly like me, but Kiko knew what was up. Fake Melony stood in between the tree and the school. *And* she was holding hands with Miasma, of all people. I wasn't the only one who was pretty much flippin' out by this development.

"What's going on?" Evil Melony asked the group of kids coolly. She had her backpack—my backpack—slung casually over one shoulder. Miasma looked practically nauseous. Scat, who was standing behind them, oozed guilt.

"Did you just get here?" another girl asked as her eyes bugged out at the sight of Melony Yoshimura holding hands with one of the school's biggest troublemakers.

"Yeah. Oh my god, are the police here?"

The girl didn't answer, but she turned to one of her friends and whispered, "I don't think it was them. They're with Melony."

Evil Melony winked at the boys. "See? I told you I'd cover our tracks," she muttered so only they could hear. Them and us owls perched above her.

I peered inside the classroom to see if I could figure out what was going on. My view into it was super clear today— no glare at all from the sun on the window this morning. Maybe because . . .

There was no glass.

At least not in the windowpane. There was plenty of it all

over the sidewalk and frosted grass right outside the class-room. Bits of shimmering, light greenish-blue crystals strewn about like sprinkles on a cake.

Inside, there was no one. No students, no teacher, not even a class pet.

What?

The Dread Pirate R's cage was open, and the spotted bunny was nowhere to be seen.

Mr. Sutton was out in front of the school talking with a police officer. "Yes, it was like this when I got here this morn-ing. I'm often one of the first people at the school, but not today, I guess."

At that moment, Mr. Yoshida arrived with Chloë. He was on his phone. "Yes, I see her right here. . . . She seems just fine! Yep, happy to help." As soon as he ended his call, Kiko barked one short, loud "Woof!"

Chloë and her dad stopped in their tracks. ". . . Kiko?" my friend whispered, as if she were almost afraid to believe it.

Not even Evil Melony could keep Kiko away at this point. A ball of fur burst from the woods near the school and hur-tled toward his family.

"Oh my god, Kiko? Kiko, is that you?" My friend bent down as her lost dog covered her in kisses. "Oh, you're so skinny, KeeKee. Why'd you run away?"

"Kiko, buddy, where ya been?" Mr. Yoshida looked as happy and relieved as Chloë did.

"Woof!" he barked. "Woof! Woof!" Kiko jumped and spun and flattened his ears like an airplane to show just how happy he was.

"Sorry," Chloë's dad laughed. "I don't know what that means, but I'm so glad you're back."

"Tell them, Kiko," I shouted. "Tell them how you got home!"

Kiko's ears perked at the sound of my hoots and he ran toward the tree where Jun and I perched. He barked up at us and then dashed back toward Mr. Yoshida. Again, he ran toward the tree and barked.

Melony's eyes followed Kiko. She let go of Miasma's hand and hunkered down to extend an open palm to Kiko. "Here, pup," she said, trying to coax him away from the tree. "Want some pets?" She smiled in her sweet, deceptive way.

But Kiko was not to be fooled. His lips curled and the fur raised on his back. He snarled at Evil Melony.

"Kiko, no! What's gotten into you?" Chloë's dad scolded their dog. "He must still be on edge after having been lost for so long," Mr. Yoshida apologized. "Sorry he's being like this!"

"That's okay, Mr. Yoshida!" Evil Melony observed Kiko coolly while my friend Chloë watched *her* with narrowed eyes.

"By the way, your parents just called." Mr. Yoshida looked at Melony with concern. "Everything okay? They didn't know where—"

Screeeech! At that moment, my parents' car careened into

the parking lot and skidded to a stop. My mom and dad ran out from the vehicle toward the one they thought was their daughter.

"Melony. Melony! Oh, thank goodness you're safe." They waved and shouted in Japanese. "Where have you been? Was it the Amanjaku? Are you all right?"

Evil Melony looked relieved that Chloë and her dad's attention was now on my parents, but she also seemed nervous when my parents mentioned the Amanjaku.

"What did they say?" Chloë whispered to her dad.

Mr. Yoshida shook his head. "Not sure, but I think they're trying to warn her about something."

Chloë looked disappointed.

Her dad sighed. "I know, I know, I really should have tried to learn more Japanese when I was a kid," he admitted.

"Now!" Jun urged me. "Everyone is here. They all sense something. You must make them see who you are—who you *really* are—go!" With that, Jun pushed me out of the tree. I spread my wings and glided above them.

Woof! Woof, woof! Kiko looked up at me and barked. His tail wagged like a windshield wiper during a rainstorm.

I circled. "That's right, Kiko! It's me," I hooted. "Help me! Can you convince everyone that I'm me?"

Kiko grinned again and jumped into a play bow as I landed on the jungle gym. He wiped at his muzzle with his paw, just like he did the first time we met.

"That!" My parents pointed at me. "*That* is the Amanjaku!"

"The owl?" Mr. Yoshida asked. "Is that what 'amanjaku' means?"

"No!" My father sounded exasperated. "In Japan, there are tales about the Amanjaku, which is kind of like an evil spirit, a demon—"

My mom jumped in to add, "We know this sounds hard to believe, but—"

My best friend looked straight at me.

Make the connection, Chloë! I bobbed and nodded. *Make the connection!*

"Kiko did that when he first met Melony." She remembered.

"Did what?" my father asked.

Kiko swiped at his nose one more time with his paw.

"This is it!" A hoot from a nearby tree filled me with excitement. Jun hopped from branch to branch as he urged me on.

"This is it, let them know! Tell them who you are!"

I took a deep breath and knew what I needed to do.

With my wings tucked in at my sides I flew like an arrow toward Evil Melony. Since her backpack was just over one shoulder like how all the cool kids carried theirs, this made it easier for me to grasp it with my talons and pull it away.

It was too heavy for me to carry far. Still, I was able to fly it a few feet away where I tore at it with my beak until I found what I was looking for—Mr. Sutton's fountain pen. I grasped it in a talon and flew straight toward him. He ducked and covered his head with his hands. I dropped the pen on the sidewalk in front of him with a clatter. Then I glided back into the tree to gather my breath.

Mr. Sutton picked up his pen and stood up slowly. He seemed confused as he looked at the Amanjaku as if he were seeing it for the first time. ". . . Melony?"

The Amanjaku answered back, its voice like mine but also not. "I have *no* idea how it got there."

My mom, my dad, and the growing crowd of students and parents who had arrived at school murmured and whispered. They seemed unconvinced.

Out of the corner of my eye, I heard a rustle and spotted a flash of white fluff in the bushes nearby. Again, I leapt out of the tree.

My classmates gasped as I emerged into the sky with a wriggling, terrified class bunny in my grasp.

Miasma screamed, "No!"

"The owl! It's going to eat the Dread Pirate R!" Scat joined in.

I don't know if I could have eaten the Dread Pirate R if I wanted to. His confined life in his class cage with Miasma and Scat and—without a doubt—many other students sneaking him treats throughout the day had made him quite plump. In fact, I was having a hard time even carrying him!

I flew right over the boys and dropped the bunny into Scat's arms. For a moment, he merely stood there looking stunned over what had just happened. I swooped back into the fir tree.

"Oh, thank goodness." Mr. Sutton rushed over and gently took the Dread Pirate R from Scat. "You wouldn't happen to know how he got out?" our teacher asked. His voice was stern but not unkind.

"I . . ." Scat glanced over at Evil Melony and then back toward Mr. Sutton. "We *talked* about letting him go."

"Jay, didn't you hear what I said about how dangerous—"

"I might have said that I wanted to free it, but it was Melony who—"

"What?" Evil Melony backed up. "*You're* the one who wished he had more freedom," she added defensively. "I just helped that wish come true."

"So, you . . . ?" Mr. Sutton asked Melony. "*You* did this too?" He gestured toward the broken window. "Melony, what's gotten into you?"

Slowly, Miasma, Scat, my parents, Mr. Yoshida, and Chloë formed a circle around Evil Melony. I held my breath, waiting and hoping beyond hope that *someone* would finally connect the dots.

My mom went first.

"Melony serves me tea when she senses I'm stressed," she said, her eyes panicked as she took a step toward the Amanjaku. "You didn't, not once, over this past week."

"I thought you didn't notice," I hooted to my mom. I felt my heart skip a beat when I realized that she had.

"Melony always plays the potato chip game," my dad added. "I know she thinks it's silly, but she does it because she knows it brightens my day. *You* said you were too old for it now." My dad closed in on the Amanjaku too.

You're wrong, I sent my thoughts toward my dad. *I play it because I like the potato chip game. I like playing this game with you.*

"Melony could tell how hard it was to be the new kid, so she became my friend even though I could tell she was okay being alone. She bought me a lollipop from the PTA fundraiser. *You*"—Chloë pointed her finger accusingly at the Amanjaku—"*you* only care about being with the cool kids. And as much as you want to be part of them, you want to feel better than them too."

"Having you as a friend was way better than being alone," I told Chloë using my owl words. She didn't turn my way, so I know I was just background noise to her, but I said them anyway. "I hope we can be friends again."

Mr. Sutton looked down at his pen. He twirled it once, twice. "I would never in my wildest dreams believe that Melony Yoshimura would steal something of mine. Let alone break into the school. At least, not the Melony I know."

When my favorite teacher of all time said this, on top of everything else people had declared, I wanted to cry. And even though owls don't have tear ducts, I felt a drip of moisture trickle down my face and past my nose.

Still, the Amanjaku looked exactly like me. I held out my

arm, but it was still the wing of an owl.

What else did I need to do?

"Melony didn't like me. *At* all." To my surprise, Miasma chimed in as well. "To be honest, I don't know why you decided that you do." He spoke directly to Evil Melony. "At least to act like you do."

Suddenly, I came up with an idea. I hooted, "Who-who-who. Wh-wh-wh-who, wh-wh-wh-who." It was the rhythm for the special ensemble audition piece: *tri-pl-et, one-ee-and-ah, two-ee-and-ah.* I repeated, "Who-who-who. Wh-wh-wh-who, wh-wh-wh-who."

"Wait." Miasma's body straightened as if my tune had put him on alert. "Where do I know that beat from?"

Excited that he heard me, I repeated, "Who-who-who. Wh-wh-wh-who, wh-wh-wh-who."

"That's . . . Is that from—?" Miasma was close—*so close!*—to making the connection.

"Who-who-who. Wh-wh-wh-who, wh-wh-wh-who!" I hooted so hard that I felt lightheaded.

Then, finally, Miasma looked up into the tree at me—*right at me*—and asked, ". . . Melony?"

I decided then and there that if I ever got back to being myself again, I wouldn't call him Miasma anymore. Even to myself.

The circle that everyone had formed around Evil Melony tightened.

Grrrr . . . Kiko snarled and snapped at the Amanjaku, who, curiously, looked less like me than before. Maybe it was something in the eyes, or maybe its arms looked longer, its nails sharper than I remembered mine being. But instead of taking a step toward Evil Melony like the others had done, Kiko suddenly bolted toward the base of the tree where I was perched. He grabbed one of my plumes that had fallen to the ground and spun in circles, chasing his tail and kicking up evergreen needles, gravel, and feathers. When he stopped, he panted at everyone, then put his paws at the base of the tree. He barked at me as he wagged his tail furiously.

"Good boy, Kiko," I hooted. "Well done."

"When I went to Jun's funeral, I stayed for some time afterward at his grave. I couldn't believe he was gone," my dad rasped as he stared at Evil Melony. "There was a raven that cawed at me the entire time. I told it to go away, even threw a rock at it. But it came back."

Evil Melony tensed as she locked eyes with my father.

Then, he looked up in the tree where Jun and I were perched. Everyone else turned to see where he was looking.

"Melony? That's you, isn't it?"

He saw me! They all *saw* me as I really am.

It is! It is! I wanted to hoot back.

But I didn't, because at that moment, Fake Melony was gone, and in her place was a scowling, furry demon—the Amanjaku as it had first appeared to me. Only this time, there was nothing harmless about its appearance. Its teeth were bared and claws exposed. And it was lunging toward my father's back.

"Noooooo!!!" I shrieked as I swooped out of the tree, determined to protect my family and everyone else I cared about from this demon once and for all.

Only I didn't fly this time.

Arms had replaced wings as I plummeted toward the earth and the pile of feathers that my former owl body had been reduced to.

Before my world turned black, I found myself wishing—hoping—I had done enough to protect them from the Amanjaku.

Chapter TWENTY-FIVE

My world was dark and full of nothing. Nothing at all. Can a world be full of nothing? Or would that make it empty of everything?

But then there were sparks of light. As I approached, I realized they were stars. My world was no longer filled with nothing.

A rustle of feathers was the first sound to enter my world.

Then an owl. He flapped toward the twinkling in the darkness.

Hoot, hoot, he added. *I'm free.*

Thank you, Jun, I responded without words. I watched as he flew past me and away.

I don't know why I didn't follow, why I *couldn't* follow.

All I could do was observe as he disappeared, leaving only a trail of stardust where he used to be.

My world was a blackness I floated in. Rushing sounds

like a river, a bump, and a jostle. Then a *crack!* and a sliver of light so blindingly bright. Two faces peering down on me. A mother. A father. *My* mother and father.

The silvery notes of their voices falling down on me like gentle rain. "A baby girl? Oh, our wish has come true! How fortunate we are, how we have wanted you for so long."

Beep . . . beep.

This unnatural sound—so strangely out of place where I was—pulled at me.

Beep . . . beep.

The empty world I was suspended in was now above me, and the stars very much out of reach.

Beep.

I awoke to the noise of a machine next to my bed. Not *my* bed, actually, but a bed that I was in.

Owls don't sleep in beds.

I tried to get up at this realization, but I was sore, and I couldn't use my arm to push myself from my prone position. It was encased in a stiff, heavy splint.

Hands rushed to ease me back down, to fluff up my pillows. A worn, faded blanket with a watermelon pattern was brought up close to my face and tucked under my chin.

Then there was a *buzz, buzz* as the back of my bed lifted slowly so I was now sitting somewhat upright.

"Otousan!" my mom called out. "Uriko okita yo!"

Steps rushing toward me and then two sets of eyes peering down on me. A mother. A father. Older than in my dream, but it was them—*my* mother and father. A cool hand on my forehead.

"Uriko, we were so worried!" my dad said.

"What happened?" I rasped. White, white, everything here was white. So different from the darkness I fell into.

"You fell from the persimmon tree and broke your arm," my mom explained.

"And got a concussion," my dad added as he adjusted my old baby blanket around me. "Mr. Chase found you on the ground beneath it and rushed you here."

I still felt groggy and disoriented. "Mr. who?" I asked.

"Mr. Chase," my mom repeated. "Our backyard neighbor. You know, the one whose tree you fell out of?"

I blinked, then remembered. "The mean one?"

My mom looked sheepish. "No, Mr. Chase—John—is actually very kind. He's been quite worried about you, you know! He sent those."

A pile of delicious plump orange persimmons sat inside a cream-colored bowl decorated with bright blue swirls. Despite all the trouble they had caused, I started to drool.

But wait—did she say *when* I fell from the tree in our neighbor's yard? Because last I remembered, I fell from a tree at school. . . .

Before I could ask any questions to clear up what exactly had happened, there was a knock on the door and then a familiar voice.

"May we come in?" It was Chloë's.

A third set of eyes and now a fourth were down peering at me. My friend held a black-and-white stuffed-animal owl in her arms. It had a bright red bow tied around it with a cheerful yellow card tucked beneath the ribbon. Mrs. Yoshida was with her too.

"The owl's from us, but the card is from the class." Chloë seemed unsure as she took a step away from my bed. She looked up at my parents and whispered, "Is she going to be back at school soon?"

"Yes, by next week, I believe!" I was as relieved to hear my father say this as Chloë must have been. "Her arm still needs to be set properly, but the doctors said she could go back after that."

"Thank goodness!" Mrs. Yoshida added. "We were so worried."

I lifted my unbroken arm to accept the owl. I stared into its plastic eyes, still trying to make sense of what did (or didn't?) happen.

Chloë broke out into a smile. "It's been no fun without you," she told me.

"Thanks," I replied. "I'll be happy to be back too."

"You wouldn't believe what's been going on while you've been away." She talked quickly, like the words had been pent up behind a dam and had to burst through. "You know the Dread Pirate R? Well, he went *missing*, and it turned out that Miasma and Scat—" At this point, Chloë paused to make sure her mom hadn't been listening.

Turns out she was, and she conveyed everything she wanted to say with a sharply raised right eyebrow.

"I mean, *Hunter and Jay*," Chloë corrected herself with an eye roll, "had planned a jailbreak for it—"

"Oh yeah?" I sat up. This all sounded *so familiar*.

"And it actually was bouncing around outside. But believe it or not, an *owl* brought it back!"

"You mean like . . . ?" I flapped the wings of the stuffed bird on my lap.

"Yeah, but I'm thinking the Dread Pirate R was too big for the owl to carry it because it ended up *dropping it on top of Jay*. Or was it Hunter?" Chloë tilted her head to the side to think for a moment.

So, it wasn't a dream? I wondered. But she didn't mention a word about my role—or Evil Melony's role—in any of this. She didn't say anything about a demon who looked like me suddenly not looking like me and lunging to attack my dad.

I would think those were important details she wouldn't leave out if they had happened.

Chloë stayed and chatted about other goings-on at Rose-creek, but I must admit, I didn't hear a lot of what she said. I closed my eyes. It was all a bit too complicated to figure out at the moment.

After a few minutes, a nurse arrived and Chloë left with her mom. My friend wanted to stay a little longer, but Mrs. Yoshida explained, "We have to let Melony get some rest! She's been through quite the ordeal."

You can say that again! I thought to myself as they departed. Although I was happy to see Chloë, I was also tired again, *really* tired.

I breathed a sigh of relief, finally feeling like the Amanjaku—whether it was real or it was not—no longer had a hold of me anymore.

Chapter TWENTY-SIX

"AAAAAIIIIIEEEEE!"

Chloë and I both screamed when a zombie appeared around a corner in the movie we were watching. We shrieked again when the family ran inside an abandoned store to hide, only to realize there were *even more* undead monsters hanging out in the cereal aisle. I hid behind my pillow, but Chloë didn't take her eyes off the screen.

"Come on!" She tugged at my pillow. "You're missing the best part!"

Since my right arm was still weak, I quickly lost our tug-of-war battle. Chloë tossed my cushion behind the sofa right as a zombie came within inches of the girl who was trying to escape it.

"Noooooo!!!" I screamed again.

"I still don't understand why you two wanted to watch this." My mom poked her head out from the dining room.

"You know you're going to have nightmares for weeks now. Chloë-chan." My mom turned to my friend. "You're such a nice girl—why do you like such terrifying things?"

Chloë laughed. "Horror movies are like roller coasters," she explained. "They might be scary while they're happening, but they're also exciting, and in the end we're all safe and sound."

"Hmm." My mom didn't sound convinced. "I don't know about that. I've heard of several unfortunate accidents involving roller coasters—"

At this point, I paused the movie we were watching and shot my mom a look. She cleared her throat. "But you're right, what's the harm in a scary movie?"

I pressed "play," but not before I heard my mother mumble, "I still don't understand, but oh well."

Things were different after my fall.

When I asked if I could have this sleepover, there were no objections from my parents, no explanations about how "sleepovers aren't something Japanese kids have." Instead, they made sure we had enough popcorn, but popped on the stove top and not in a microwaved bag. "Tastes better and it's healthier," my dad explained. Over the kernels, he sprinkled some wasabi nori flavoring that he had brought back from the potato chip factory.

It had been over a month since my arm was taken out of its cast and even longer since I had been discharged from the hospital. During that time, there hadn't been a single mention of Evil Melony and how badly she behaved. Dad's potato chip collection was gone ("It was attracting so many ants!" he explained). I also had the fancy notebook that Chloë had given me, but other than that, it wasn't clear to me how many of my adventures with the Amanjaku had happened or not.

But one thing was for certain. I had a little more freedom than before, and I wasn't quite sure why. The shirt with the slashes in it was still in my closet, along with the ripped jeans. I tried them on again one afternoon to see if they were actually real. My mother didn't even ask when I had bought them, although I did see her raising an eyebrow skeptically at my outfit. The twelve-dollar boots that I'd only paid $8.40 for were nowhere to be found, though. Could it be because I paid for the clothes fair and square, but the boots came about from the Amanjaku's deceptive ways? I wasn't certain if I'd ever know for sure.

Now that my arm had healed, I was starting to play the piccolo again. But I had lost weeks of practice, so Hunter took my place in the special ensemble. Part of me still wished to go on the band trip, but another part wanted to earn my spot through my own effort. I told my parents I would skip it this spring. After all, Ms. Delgado said there would be another trip next year. And I *knew* I'd be better than Hunter by then.

Speaking of the boys I used to call Miasma and Scat, things were the same, and different, at school too. Hunter and Jay were less obnoxious. *Slightly.* Granted, they had to stay after school for almost a month and help Mr. Sutton clean his classroom every day. But maybe that extra time with an understanding teacher was actually just what they needed. On my first day back in class, the Dread Pirate R was no longer there. He had been moved to Mr. Sutton's parents' farm.

"I agree with what Hunter and Jay had said about his cage being too small," our teacher explained to the class. "And now our rabbit has lots of room to roam in his new home. I'll try to bring him back on occasion." While we were disappointed we wouldn't get to see our class pet every day, we were happy that he had more than two hops' worth of space to live.

Chloë really had lost her first phone and so she did have a new one. She explained that it happened before my fall— "Don't you remember?" she asked. I blamed temporary amnesia as a result of my accident, which she seemed to buy. But that all-encompassing wish to have a phone of my own was gone. I had no idea where Chloë's old phone went, or if I'd even had it in the first place. Did I still want one? Sure! Would I be willing to repeat everything that happened to get one? No flippin' way!

But it wasn't like everything was perfect now, especially me. The other day, I wanted to go hang out with Chloë and my mom said, "Not until you finish your trash chore."

"I'll do it when I get back," I replied without thinking.

She got really quiet and asked me to reflect a second on my response. Then I realized—my chore was to gather all the trash from inside the house and put it in the bin, and my dad's was to roll out the bin. If I didn't do my part, he couldn't do his. What I did and how I acted affected other people.

This was just one example, but if there's one thing the Amanjaku taught me, it's that telling yourself, "It's not like I'm hurting anyone" isn't always true. When I was lying in the hospital, I heard my dad mutter to my mom, "She has to be okay. She has to! What would we do without her?" I understood then that it wasn't such a bad thing to have people who cared for you so much. Of course, wishes are fine—everyone has them, and everyone should. It wasn't a bad thing for me to wish for more freedom, but now I realized it also came with responsibility.

When the zombie movie ended, Chloë and I brought up our empty bowls to the kitchen sink, washed them, and put them away. As she went to brush her teeth, I prepared a cup of tea for my mom. She was humming quietly to herself in the dining room as she worked on her newest creation.

"Pata pata pat-tan, tat-ton ton.

Pata pata pat-tan, tat-ton ton."

I carried the cup toward the dining room slowly so I wouldn't spill a drop.

I almost let it crash to the floor, though, when I saw what

she was working on.

There, on the dining room table, was the most amazing, colorful quilt I'd ever seen my mother put together.

In each patch was a picture made from scraps of patterned cloth . . . that illustrated an adventure that the Amanjaku and I had.

The box labeled *Uriko* that arrived on our porch.

Two girls eating a pile of cookies in the kitchen.

Two music stands with drawings scribbled in silver marker over them.

The pair of fleece-lined boots it convinced me to buy.

A girl peering into her phone, but the reflection in the screen was that of the Amanjaku.

Ripe orange persimmons at the top of a tree against a bright blue sky.

An owl silhouetted in the light of a full moon.

I stood there speechless for I don't know how long.

Without looking up, my mother asked, "Is that for me?"

My hands shook as I set the cup down with a rattle. My mom took it and sipped. "Thank you, Uriko."

Hearing her use my old name snapped me out of my silence. "Mom, you said the Amanjaku was the reason you guys left Japan. Why . . . why would you make a whole quilt about it?"

I wanted to ask more, like *Did everything really happen? How did you know about these events? Aren't you scared you're going to invite it in?*

But before I could get the words out, my mom answered. "There is much to be frightened of in this world. But less when we face it and conquer it together, don't you think? Accomplishments should be celebrated and acknowledged. That's what this does."

So it all happened! I wanted to shout. But what she said next made me question myself again.

"Plus, the Amanjaku is just an old wives' tale." My mom smoothed out the quilt and admired her own handiwork.

Once more, I doubted whether she in fact knew the whole story.

"Okaasan," my dad called out to my mom from the desk in the kitchen where he sat looking at the computer. "I found some good fares to Japan. Do you think . . ." He paused for a moment as that sad, faraway look passed over his eyes, but only for a second. "Do you think it's time to go back for a visit this spring?"

Mom and I peered over my dad's shoulder. "Those *are* good fares. Maybe we could go during cherry blossom season," she mused. Then she peered out the window. "Look at how bright the moon is tonight."

My dad and I both turned our heads. We've had this ongoing disagreement about what we see in the moon. My parents said that, like all Japanese people, they saw a rabbit first and foremost. I'd always seen a man and I had no problem telling them so.

Tonight, though, there was not only a man in the moon, but he resembled the potato chip that reminded my dad of Jun. But, unlike in the chip, his face was broad and smiling and I knew that he was finally free.

"How interesting!" my mother exclaimed. "Tonight, I *do* see a man."

"Do you think . . . ?" My dad's voice trailed off as he stared at the moon without saying whether he saw a man or a rabbit.

"We can visit Jun," I finished for him.

He looked surprised at my suggestion, but then he nodded. "Yes, it would be good to pay our respects at his grave."

My heart sank at my father's comment. I wished I'd imagined my father mentioning Jun's funeral during our confrontation with the Amanjaku.

But part of me knew deep down inside that he was gone and no longer of this world.

Later that night, or more like the early, early morning, Chloë lay snoring in her sleeping bag on the floor while I lay awake in my bed reliving everything that had or hadn't happened in the past few months. I came to the conclusion that my parents knew on some subconscious level what had taken place. But maybe their memories were like the bark of a tree when moss grew, covering them up when the Amanjaku lost its hold over me.

Tap, tap, tap. Tappity, tap, tap.

I had dozed off, but my eyes opened all of a sudden at the sound of a tree branch knocking—not on my window but somewhere down the hall.

"Who, who, who, whoooo? Who, who, who, whoooo?"

I sat up straight at the call of the barred owl and tiptoed out of bed. At least I thought I did, but when I looked back over my shoulder, there I was—still sound asleep.

I was past the point of being amazed at anything that happened, but I was still determined to see who was outside. I slipped quietly down the dark and silent hallway. My feet didn't make a sound, not even on the floorboard that creaked whenever I stepped on it.

I stood at the kitchen window and waited as I stared into the pitch black.

Just a few seconds later, the face of an owl appeared within inches of mine.

At first, my heart leapt with gratitude to see my friend Jun again. I had never thanked him for his help. But then I remembered my happiness at watching him flying into the moon, knowing that at long last he was free.

But when it stared at me with accusing, glowing eyes, I knew exactly who this was.

"Who?" it asked. "Who? Who?"

I met its angry gaze and gathered my thoughts before I answered. "I am Uriko Melony Yoshimura. *I* am me, and I will never let *you* be me again."

The owl was silent for what seemed like an eternity. Then

it replied with short rapid hoots, like it was laughing. "Fine, then. I'll find someone else to let me in."

"Everyone here knows to avoid you," I answered. "And if they don't, I'll tell them." I crossed my arms and waited to see how it would react. "I guess you're gonna have to go pretty far away to find anyone who doesn't know about you."

As the owl and I faced off, its eyes seemed to dim and the fierce glow behind them faded. "Guess I will. . . . Guess I will," it hooted softly, then it turned and took off silently into the night sky.

But maybe I dreamed this final meeting with the Amanjaku. Maybe this was nothing more than a nightmare from watching scary movies before bed. Or maybe, like with everything that had happened the past few months, I'd never be able to determine what was real, what wasn't, and what fell somewhere in between. But no matter what did or didn't happen, a few things I knew for sure . . . I would always make a wish on my birthday, but I'd be careful never to let an unfortunate one take control of my life again.

And I would savor every single bite of that cake.

Author's NOTE

"Urikohime to Amanjaku" ("The Melon Princess and the Amanjaku") was one of my favorite stories growing up. In fact, it was mentioned in the first chapter of my memoir, *While I Was Away*, and I still have my copy of this childhood favorite on my desk. The version of this folktale that I grew up with was quite simple: An elderly couple prays to the gods for a child, and the gods, in turn, send them a melon. After retrieving it from the river, the old woman takes the melon home and cuts it open. To her and her husband's surprise, a baby is inside! They name her Uriko, and treasure and take care of her, but (in my five-year-old mind) they really *were* quite overprotective—they wouldn't let her do anything! One day, the parents leave for town and urge Uriko not to open the door for anyone. At this point, the demon Amanjaku (sometimes referred to as Amanojaku) appears, and, of course, Uriko lets it in. They have a grand ole time until it leaves her stranded, tied high up in a persimmon tree. When Uriko's parents return, they panic because they cannot find their daughter anywhere. A raven, however, informs them of Uriko's whereabouts. After rescuing her, Uriko's parents forgive her because *anyone* who encounters the Amanjaku wants to go places they've never been, taste food they've never tasted, and see things they wouldn't have seen otherwise. As you can see, *The Very Unfortunate Wish of Melony Yoshimura* has incorporated many elements of the folktale . . . and added many others for a contemporary American twist!

Clearly, I was obsessed with this story because I relished the freedom Uriko enjoyed on that afternoon her parents were away and the adventures she experienced thanks to the Amanjaku. However, in researching this tale a bit further, I discovered it had a much darker side. The Amanjaku is actually an evil spirt or demon that has the ability to (1) mimic and appear as other people and things, and (2) awaken people's darkest desires and compel them to commit wicked deeds in order to fulfill them. In some versions of the story, the Amanjaku kills Uriko and masquerades as her until the village comes together to defeat it.

Although my Japan-born-and-raised parents believe they were quite lenient with me, in comparison to my more "American" friends, they, like Uriko's parents, were quite protective and strict. Good grades and behavior were, of course, a given. Above all else, they believed in education, hard work, and following the rules as the recipe for success and a stable way of life. There were many aspects of the US that they enjoyed; however, there were also many that were suspect, because "that would never happen in Japan." Anything that was "too American" in their eyes was viewed as a possible corrupting influence. In talking with many of my friends who are children of immigrant parents, I found this was a common theme in their lives as well.

Generational tension is common among many families. However, with immigrant families, there's also a cultural tension. When thinking about the Amanjaku, who tries to imitate and pass itself off as other people and things, it struck me that not only did I identify with the sheltered Uriko who longed to go out and have adventures, but I—as well as many children of immigrants—identified with the Amanjaku and its ability to shape-shift, in a sense, to fit the ideas and expectations of others around us.

I continue to relate to Uriko's story, but this time more as a parent as I raise my own children. In terms of why I felt compelled to write this reimagining of Uriko/Melony's tale now, I am noticing with my children, other parents, and the world in general that there is a high degree of anxiety and fear of the outside world. And rightly so! The COVID-19 health crisis coupled with the tween years in which children seek their independence (and my hesitance to give it to them as a parent) can result in some tense interactions. However, like many other families, my own boys, my husband, and I have been doing our best to manage our concerns together.

Spooky stories such as Melony's are often about conquering fears. At this point in time, in which I'm writing this author's note, unfortunately we are still in the midst of this harrowing pandemic. Just as Melony does in her journey, it is my fervent wish that we can reconcile our own feelings of fear, desire for freedom, and responsibility toward others and become better people for it as we move forward.

Acknowledgments

People often think of writing as a solitary endeavor, but having a book published is not. It takes a team, and I'm very fortunate to have so many people who support me and the stories I create.

I'm extremely grateful for my editor, Alyssa Miele, and everyone at Quill Tree Books/HarperCollins for taking Melony's story on. Even though it's admittedly *quite* different from my first two books, Alyssa graciously and expertly guided me throughout the process as we worked together to bring the best version of Melony's tale to life. It's often hard for me to believe how lucky I've been to land at Quill Tree and to have Alyssa as my editor.

Even before presenting *The Very Unfortunate Wish of Melony Yoshimura* to my publisher, I worked with my brilliant agent, Penny Moore, through several drafts of my proposal. I'm fortunate to have an agent who is so fantastic at her job.

I appreciate your dedication and advice so much!

I'm in awe of the beautiful cover that Shoko Ishida created. Many thanks to her for capturing the essence of Melony's adventures. Additional thanks to Erin Fitzsimmons, who designed the book's jacket and interior, and to Mikayla Lawrence, Ivy McFadden, Sonja West, and Gweneth Morton for their copyediting and proofreading of this novel.

I would also like to extend my gratitude to the many people who read earlier versions of this story and offered feedback throughout. To my longstanding writing group, John, Matt, and Aileen—I'm so happy we were able to meet in person again during the early stages of this novel. Even though the pretzels we consumed were stale, our conversations and the laughs certainly were not!

All writers need someone in their corner like Haris Leventi. Haris's praise and friendship offered me much-needed encouragement during the ups and downs of writing this story. To my young readers Zoe Li and Adelle Tyner, thank you for taking the time to read early drafts and provide your valuable thoughts and suggestions. My books are for children like you, so your approval filled me with happiness. I also greatly appreciate Mr. Isao Nakazawa for answering my questions about some of the Japanese used in this book.

To my own children, Kogen, Tai, and Leo. I couldn't have asked for a better trio of boys to call my own. If you turned into owls, I bet I'd recognize you guys right away!

Writers who juggle work and family know that a supportive

spouse makes a sometimes-stressful process so much easier. When I had deadlines, my husband, Miles—without question or complaint—handled any family and household duties that I wasn't able to. When there was a crisis, he resolved it. Miles is truly our superhero.

Finally, this story would never have come to pass if it weren't for my parents. To my father, who told me the original folktale of the Melon Princess more times than I can count, and to my mother, who fixed our dinners while I was being read to—thank you for everything.